The Scarlet Scarf

By: David G. Woods

Acknowledgements:

I would like to thank all those who helped me in the writing of this book. It truly was a collaboration of friends. A special thanks goes to my wife Darlene Woods, you keep us all well fed. I would also like to thank Ruth Kubeja for all of your countless hours of editing. Last but not least I would like to thank Roberta Carlson for you technical and collaborative support.

CHAPTER ONE

It was a cool, crisp fall day in the early 20s that Paula and Jim were left home with their baby sitter while their parents had gone to a meeting at the church, although young at the time Jim remembers the ride to the crash site where his parents the Williams were lying dead on the road. From that moment on it seemed like a whirlwind of activity. He also remembered Paula being anxious about their fate and crying in fear of them being split apart. He also felt that their parents must have been watching over them. When his aunt and uncle sent for them from Canada,

    They were a vivacious couple who loved to be around children, playing with an interacting with them in their community also their church groups. Eagerly took over the activities along with the responsibilities of bringing up their niece and nephew from America. They were unable to have children of their own.

Shortly after the funeral was over Paula and Jim were on their way to Canada. Jim was enrolled in school where he was quick to catch on excelling in his studies. He was very mechanically inclined was always helping his uncle around the farm. Jim enjoyed most of his life in Canada however he and Paula always had the urge to return to America. Paula went to work at a local hotel about 20 min. from the farm to help out with expenses. She was part of the housekeeping staff. Basic tear down and redressing rooms but would also help in the pub when needed. She rarely noticed any one of the opposite sex.

However, from time to time, she noticed a slender decorated Pilot from the German Army would stop at the hotel. She wondered to her self maybe he was some kind of double agent. He was very tall, blue eyes, blonde hair cut short in true military style. Paula was a very beautiful young girl, blonde hair, blue eyes with an early maturing body, but she was able to retain her innocence. Maybe that's why some men were attracted to her several of them had approached her about dating. She had never quite thought about it. Her life had been quite chaotic, since her mother and father died and they had moved to Canada. She gave little thought to dating. One day while she was working in the pub. This German officer approached her introducing himself as Wolfgang. He had been seen quite often with younger women He seem to be the life of the party, with an unlimited supply of money. He liked to spend it on women, mostly under the age of 20. As he approached Paula She became leery of him but Wolfgang seemed to calm her by his general conversation Paula, would you be so kind as to accompany me for a drink. The words slithered from Wolfgang's lips with a sly ominous tone. He had never been rejected by woman before and confident that he would not be turned down this night. Paula somewhat honored that a soldier would pay any attention to her so she politely accepted Wolfgang's offer. He went to the bar ordered two drinks then turned to face the other patrons in the bar. The bartender also the owner had seen Wolfgang in there before having his way with local women, especially young women, the bartender took advantage of Wolfgang's lack of interest in his preparation of the drinks he watered them down in fact, there was no alcohol at all in Paula's drink He reluctantly handed the drinks to Wolfgang never taking his eyes off them, to the owner's surprise after only one drink Wolfgang seemed to lose interest and abruptly turned his interest to some other young lady at the bar. Not knowing that Wolfgang had asked her to join him in his room for more drinks. She had refused and he did not like that.

Shortly after she left the hotel, there was only about 10 min. left in her walk home, the road lit up behind her. She heard a car door, then turned to see Wolfgang, with one cruel motion he threw her to the ground ripping at her clothing then while she whimpered he took her innocence in one horrific act of his own personal gratification. Then as he left laughing to himself, she deserved it. That girl should have never taunted me or turned down my advances. Paula crying and violated stood up quickly in disbelief she gathered up her things off the ground, sill crying she noticed a swath of red cloth that didn't belong to her. She stuffed it in her pocket then trying to arrange her clothing that he had torn, continued her walk home still crying wondering why anybody could be so cruel. When Paula got home she told her aunt of the horrific act that had befallen her. Her aunt openly wept with her then helped her clean up and sat with her until she fell asleep. Her aunt told her uncle in detail of what had happened. Paula did not know till much later that her uncle tried to find Wolfgang, but to no avail. When Paula woke up the next day, trying to make sense of what happened the previous night. She was putting her clothes away when she noticed the piece of cloth that was sticking out of her coat pocket, pulled it out. It was a hand knitted Scarlett Scarf. She found a shoebox, with anger and crying she stuffed the scarf in the box then put it under her bed, feeling sick to her stomach went to the bathroom to throw up. Paula was not permitted to return to work at the hotel. Her uncle had a great fear that Wolfgang would return After a few weeks Paula realize she was feeling something unusual. After speaking to her aunt about this she discovered that she was with child. Paula wept as did her aunt. Her uncle vowed to keep her on the farm for fear that there would be public ridicule of his beloved niece and her child, he insisted that she kept her unborn child, he told her that she would not be able to bear life without the love of this child, regardless of the circumstances, this child would belong to her and no one else. He told her she may never be able to love a man, after what had happened to her or find a man that would accept her and her child. Some people would consider Paula as a shamed woman, not knowing what really had happened.

On a spring day Paula gave birth to a son with the help of her aunt. He had blue eyes, blonde hair His name was Jim, after her brother, because he had been a great help and she hoped this child would grow up to be like him but they would call him Buddy.

As he grew up Jim became a father figure to him. Every ball game Cub Scout meeting he was always there to offer Buddy his guidance Jim also passed on his life's passion of flying and airplanes. Shortly after Jim graduated from school He applied at several American aircraft manufacturers. Curtiss aircraft plant offered Jim an internship almost immediately. Jim was nervous to tell Paula of his plans of moving back to America. He was also nervous that Paula would not accept his invitation to return to America with him. Jim did not know Paula's plans to one day return to her homeland again. He handed her the letter of acceptance as she read it, tears of joy welled up in her eyes, of course Jim asked if her and Buddy would come with him. Yes, she said, definitely. But how are we going to tell aunt and uncle they have been so good to us. Jim answered, saying, don't worry I will speak to our uncle tonight about this. After chores were done that evening Jim showed his uncle the letter of acceptance He also told him that Paula and Buddy would be coming with him. His uncle realized what a great opportunity this was for Jim but also was saddened of the thought of them leaving. They had become very close he would speak to their aunt about this opportunity for them. Not long afterwards, with promises of letters and pictures. Especially from Buddy growing up, the three of them were on their way back to United States.

Jim settled into his new apprenticeship quickly his supervisor recognized his talents immediately and offered him a full-time production job in record time. Jim always had time for Buddy, no matter how much time he put in at the plant they took time to go fishing and a couple of ballgames. As time went by Buddy grew tall. He would be well over 6ft.tall, with blonde hair and blue eyes he was very strong and liked working out with weights even at a young age. He was also very athletic enjoying all the sports in school. Most of all he liked running, he competed in a lot of track meets. He won quite a few, mostly he like competing against runners that were faster than him. He enjoyed the competition and the challenge, his quiet demeanor changed when he was running he was all about business, while on the track team he acquired quite a few medals however he was not boastful about his accomplishments. That's why he was so well liked in school. Both Paula and Jim were very proud of him. A lot of girls were interested in him and he dated a few, but he never could quite get serious with any one girl. When he wasn't in school or doing sports he was with his mother and his uncle. He enjoyed going to the aircraft plant, where his uncle worked. Jim had become a supervisor in research and development. This meant building new planes he had become quite a pilot himself, but his first love was developing innovations for planes that were in production to make them better when Buddy wasn't doing anything with his mother on weekends and time away from school activities. He was side-by-side with his uncle, Buddy enjoyed working on the planes, but was more interested in the flying end of it. There were occasions Jim had actually taken him up in a plane Buddy's heart would start pounding every time they went up, there was the time he asked his uncle if he could try flying so Jim let him have the controls and realized that Buddy had a real knack for controlling the planes he started showing Buddy different maneuvers. It was almost uncanny his perfection and control. It was like he was part of the plane. It got to the point where

Buddy was becoming a better pilot than Jim and not having formal training. Jim knew in his heart, where Buddy was headed. Besides his flying ability, he was able to name every plane even British and German and recite every one of their capabilities and their weakness. Jim had told Paula of Buddy's flying abilities also knowledge of airplanes so they both agreed to send Buddy to the Academy. Paula was concerned about him flying, but realized she had to let him become a man. Of course she was still very protective of him, but it was time to let him go. Then early one evening while Paula and Buddy were sitting on the front porch enjoying the evening Jim showed up with a pretty young lady. Her name was Nonny, Buddy thought he remembered her from Jim's work, so life for Jim was going to change for the better. Maybe even pull him away from the plant once in a while. At the Academy things became quite hectic with his studies. Of course, Buddy engrossed himself in all the activities he liked everything about this, it was quite strenuous at times, but then he seemed to thrive on that. The instructor who was Lt. Col. Tom Gray, everyone knew him as CT. Buddy recognized him. He was sure he saw him with his uncle at the plant several times in fact he thought that CT was from that area. He wasn't sure, but he thought that his mother CT and Jim had gone out several times. This was okay with Buddy. One thing Buddy realized CT was more critical of his work, than the other students. He wasn't sure why, but he would never complain. He knew they had to be tough on the students because it was part of their training, you better be able to handle the pressure, especially when you're flying in combat, a few men washed out, that was expected. As their training continued news from Europe would reach them. Germany was really gaining ground. They had captured France and headlines read Hitler eyes The Royal Crown. But the British were holding their ground. If Germany succeeded in capturing the British Empire they may decide to come after the United States. Buddy realized he had made a decision that when he was done and graduated he wanted to become a volunteer to help in England. They were accepting volunteer pilots, along with tanks, planes and other things to help the British fight off those Nazi thugs in Europe, Buddy realized his mother wouldn't be too happy about this, but this was his decision and he felt very strong about it. He hoped she would understand. As graduation day approached, they got a pass to leave the base and go to town. Of course, it took some persuading of his fellow students to get Buddy to go. He wasn't much of a drinker, but decided to relax and go with them. After visiting several bars which seemed to be on almost every corner. He and his friend Harry decided to head back to the base as they were walking they heard a commotion in an alley behind one of the stores. It looked like several cadets had a young girl that they were harassing, he heard her voice in distress and told Harry. Let's go see what's going on. He didn't like the looks of this as they approached one of the cadets turned saying you guys want to rumble with a laugh, six against two? What do you think Buddy was sure of himself, but he didn't know about Harry, then from the shadows behind them a voice said, how about three against six. What would you say to that then a figure stepped into the light. It was Col. Tom, when the six cadets saw this they decided not to have any part of it. They turned and fled then Harry quickly excused himself, saying he would return to base clearly shook up by this event. CT and Buddy walked the girl home. By this time, her tears had dried up, and she turned and thanked them with a smile on her face. Tom said to Buddy that was a brave thing you did, I like that in a man. Whether you know it or not, I'm sure you do. I've been rather hard on you, but I see something in you and your flying ability, I'm sure that if you stick with it, you will be a leader in time. After what I just saw what you did. I know you will be a hunter, Buddy wasn't quite sure what CT meant by that, I think I know where you get some of your flying abilities from and I know you were able to fly before you ever got here.

Thanks to your uncle at the Curtis plant, Buddy was glad that CT had not shown him any favoritism realizing now why he had been so hard on him, Buddy thanked CT with his honesty. From then on they had a special bond between them. Finally graduation day; the day they had all been looking forward to this and getting their wings also becoming officers, of course, Buddy got the highest score anybody ever got. However, he wanted that to be downplayed somewhat he felt he had the advantage the rest of the cadets didn't. That's the way he wanted things. The ceremony began with loud trumpets and traditional march down the main base road after what seemed like an eternity when Buddy's name was called. He marched up on stage where he was presented with his wings along with his Lt. bars by CT himself. He remembered looking out at the crowd, spotting his mother and Uncle Jim in the stands of course his mother was beaming and his uncle was as proud as though it was his own son. Jim had invited CT to join them after the ceremonies to spend the day with them. Of course CT jumped at the chance to spend time with them and Paula, also to hear of the latest things that was happening back home. As they set down to have supper, Buddy was a little nervous about telling them of his decision especially his mother about his plans to volunteer to go to England, and be part of the Eagle squadron. She was taken aback by this. Also, she realized that he would be going to fight the Germans, and of her past experiences were any indication of what they were like, She was afraid for Buddy. But then any mother would be with her first-hand experience with one of them. She was sure in her mind that they were not all as evil as he was, but then some of the stories that were coming out of Europe were almost unbelievable. It was hard for people of this country and their allies to understand or believe how anyone could do this to other people what was being said. Then she realized that Buddy had made his decision, and she knew no matter what was said he would not change his mind. Shortly after graduation the men got their assignments, of course, Buddy knew where he was going, so he packed his bags, then saying goodbye to his mother and his uncle Jim also CT, thanking him again, for all he had done. That's when he found out that he along with a close friend we're to fly one of the bombers to England. This was exciting for Buddy so early the next morning, they reported to the base and was assigned to a bomber that had been modified to carry some passengers of course, the excitement level was high, with the men that were going to be flying with them. So, Buddy and his copilot did their preflight. Everything checked out, and before long they were airborne headed for England

CHAPTER TWO

The flight to England was long but uneventful except for their stopover for fuel. It was good for everyone to get out and stretch their legs. This was a first time any of them had been out of America then it was back in the plane to continue their flight to their predestination in England, they were instructed to land at a base near Southampton then to be transported to their individual stations, Buddy was to report to, Whitman Castle. There he was greeted by several men. They were excited to see him one of the men took him to introduced him to his new commanding officer, Maj. Morrison their introduction was cut short by the majors preoccupation with the returning planes. The major asked Buddy to excuse him for a minute while he found out what the stats were for the mission then he gave an intense welcome to England, thanks for joining us we need all the help we can get Lieut. He turned giving orders of assignments, then he and Buddy walked out to the field, Buddy noticed several hurricanes and spitfires. The major introduced him to his flight leader, Lieut. Tim Morrison. They shook hands welcome aboard with a light smile Lieut. Harrison said to Buddy, I hope you're not looking for glory, because there is none here. Some chaps may come here looking for that, men you will meet today will be gone tomorrow. That's just the way it is here. The major said as he turned to leave, I'll let you to get acquainted. The Lieut. took Buddy to the area where his bunk was along with his locker, you may stow your stuff here, get settled in then look me up, when Buddy was done he approached the flight leader Tim Morrison who ask what would you like first, something to eat or your plane assignment, Buddy said. I'll take my plane first, the flight leader smiled, anxious to get started are you yes he replied, with that they headed out to the flight line. Some of the other planes were returning from the mission, one of the planes was setting away from the rest. It was smoking, several trucks along with an ambulance were rushing to it, Buddy wondered what the outcome would be in this case he certainly hoped it would be good also the pilot made it out safe.

Tim pointed to an airplane, Buddy said Hawker hurricane MK1 Tim nodded yes. Buddy continued, 40 feet long, wingspan 13 feet, weighs 7800 pounds loaded maximum speed 320 miles an hour has four 20 mm cannons also carries a 1000 pound bomb Tim stared in amazement. Then he said okay here is the real test, Buddy recited Spitfire MK1A powered by Rolls-Royce12 Merlin engine that produces 1,230.horse power driven by two wooden propellers puts out a top speed of 360 miles an hour it will climb 2053 feet a minute. Its armaments include Browning machine guns four on each wing and two 20 mm cannons, flight leader Tim said. Someone has done their homework. They both chuckled about that Buddy explained to the Lieut., that his uncle worked at the Curtis air plane plant in America, he had spent a lot of time there, I learned quite a bit about different airplanes. I also learned to do maintenance. I would like to try to do some of my own if it's possible with that Buddy climbed up into the plane, to check it out. The lieutenant told him to fire it up so Buddy flipped a few switches then turn it over to start the engine it coughed and sputtered a few times then came to life Buddy revved it up a few times to let it warm up, then looked down at the Lieut. and shook his head. Then he turned it off. Stepped out on the wing then on the ground saying she needs a bit of a tune up, let's go talk to the crew chief. As they approached one of the planes some men were working on, a portly man chewing on a cigar came over to them. The Lieut. introduced the two. This is officer pilot Buddy and this is crew chief Master Sgt. Axel. This is the man you want to become friends with also his crew just bring Axel, a cigar once in a while he'll be your best friend, Buddy recognize this man as a Jewish fellow, he kind of wondered how this man came to be here. It really didn't matter Axel wiped his hands on a rag sometimes in situations like this its not necessary to salute, you would much rather have them working on the planes then stop in the middle of what they were doing to salute or stand at attention every time an officer approached them.

Getting the job done was much more important Buddy spoke up, asked Axel if it was possible to do some of his own maintenance Axel looked at the flight leader so Tim explained to Axel what Buddy had told him Axel said that's fine by me. We need all the help we can get to keep these buggies in the air. I will want to know all that you do so I can keep my records straight, also I will check on you. Buddy said I appreciate that. I'm sure there's a lot to be learned. You can't learn it all from a book. I have never worked on a spitfire or hurricane, but I'm certainly willing to try Axel said well I'll have to dig up some spanners and other tools. They are not called wrenches here. The three of them chuckled about that. It was good to laugh once in a while. Then there was a sober moment when the flight leader asked how many did make it back this time Axel said we lost four and maybe the one at the end of the field. We haven't had time to check it out yet the pilot was able to bring her down but I know for sure it won't be ready for tomorrow's mission So Buddy started in on his plane, he instantly felt at home. He worked late into the evening then went back to the barracks to clean up most of the men were back by now. So he introduced himself, they were all excited to have him there and wanted to talk to him but there would be time for that later, Buddy prepared himself for the next day. It was hard for him to go to sleep thinking of what tomorrow would be like. He knew he wouldn't fail, but of coarse he had never been in combat. His biggest fear would be, to do something wrong and let his fellow pilots down. He woke sat up in bed, so he must've fell asleep at one time or another, he quickly went to the latrine to clean up realizing that it was raining and overcast. He got ready just the same, then headed to the mess hall where most every morning started, after he sat down at the table with some other men of coarse they all introduced themselves, then they asked questions about America are the people like him are they going to get more interested in the war over here? Buddy tried to answer their questions. He also expressed his wishes that they would get more involved. He explained that they are sending planes, ships, materials and volunteers. That's all I can tell you. At this time Lieut. Flight leader Harrison joined the group informing them at this time there would be no flights going up, there were foggy conditions over the area chosen for the mission today. Buddy was somewhat disappointed he was anxious to get the first combat situation over with, one of the men asked Buddy is this your first combat flight? Buddy said yes it is, the person said we've all been there, it always seems to be easier after that, but believe me it's never easy, Lieut. Harrison said to be on alert, just in case some of the Jerry's, which they called the Germans sometimes decide to come over but he doubted that they would we will be notified by our new radar site. If there's any sign of them. Buddy finished his breakfast, then headed out where the planes were, he wanted to do some more work on his, as he was working Axel approached him saying that the work Buddy had done the day before was right on the money, the more you work on your plane the better you know it, the Hurricane is not as fast or maneuverable as the Spitfire, but it will take a lot more punishment than most anything out there. I've seen these planes come back in pretty bad shape. All shot up I've even seen them come back with part of a wing missing it makes you wonder how they can keep them flying. I have a lot of respect for the hurricane. So keep this in mind, Buddy thanked him. Now I need some help. I want to set the timing and the intake Axle said I have time for that. Then I have to move on to other jobs when they were done with this Buddy fired it up, got a big smile on his face and gave a thumbs up, Axle shook his head yes and waved at him as he turned and walked back to finished doing maintenance on the other planes. He thought to himself. He wished he had time to fine-tune every plane they had, but there just wasn't time he kind of chuckled to himself maybe I could get him transferred to maintenance then laughed again. He had some great guys that worked for him. It was a great team effort to keep the birds in the air. Unknown to them Buddy and Axel both had basically the same agenda, revenge and to destroy that evil enemy that they were fighting Buddy continued working on his plane for quite some time, then realized he was hungry and headed back to the barracks to clean up, he realized the weather had changed the overcast had lifted he felt good about his plane, he was ready if they called an alert. As he entered the mess hall, gathered his food to go sit down at the table. He recognized some of the guys. Lieut. Harrison was sitting across from him. He asked Buddy what plane he had trained in, a P 38 Curtis I also was checked out in some bombers. In fact I had the chance to fly one of the bombers over here, my copilot and I brought some other pilots and personnel with us, I was kind of honored to be able to fly that large plane that distance being fresh out of the Academy. When one of the other pilots said you're quite versatile, Buddy felt a little embarrassed, he hoped he wasn't being taken for someone that brags a lot. Then, the pilot said we need more men like you. You never know when you'll be needed to fly other planes. Buddy felt a sense of pride. The lieutenant said the weather has changed how would you feel about taking your plane up for a while to get used to it, of course Buddy jumped at the chance, the lieutenant could see the anticipation on Buddy's face then gave a chuckle, so they headed out to the flight line. As they approached the planes Axel came over to ask if everything was okay. The lieutenant said yes we are going to go up so he can get familiar with the plane, probably a good idea Axle agreed, the lieutenant was flying a Spitfire, which was faster and a little easer too maneuver so they started up the planes then took off, Buddy was sure glad he made the modifications to his plane he felt it respond very quickly He was impressed with the power and handling of the hurricane. Of course, the P 38 was a trainer and this was a war machine so they played tag for a while. Buddy chased the lieutenant and realized that Lieut. Harrison was quite a flyer himself. He felt the lieutenant pushing his plane more aggressively also was glad this pilot was on our side. Buddy did his best to stay with him he wasn't sure how good he had done the lieutenant radioed to Buddy it's your turn. I'll chase you. So Buddy started his maneuvers. He was becoming very sure of his plane, he starting to push it hard. The lieutenant came over the radio very good if you have got any more, let me see it now, he was happy to oblige. He gave it everything he had, Buddy did some barrel roles, loop's also went in a tight circle. Then he did a few things that CT had shown him that may have been a little off the books things that you didn't show a regular pilot during training, but he got caught up in the moment, almost as if the enemy fighters was after him. The G forces were being felt by Buddy. He made a mental note to find a way to work out. He had not had a chance to do this while he was here. Then, over the radio the Lieut. told him to break it off. I think we've used up enough petrol. Let's put these planes back down on the ground, so they headed back down to the base landed and taxied back to where they were before. Buddy made sure everything was shut off then got down on the ground. He had a slight smile, thinking to himself. He really liked this plane. Then he walked over to the lieutenant asking if he had done okay. Lieut. Morrison's said you're more than ready for combat. I must say, I haven't seen that kind of flying from a person fresh out of flight school you possess an uncanny feel for an airplane, you fly as though you were a seasoned pilot. How did you learn some of those maneuvers did they teach you all that in flight school Buddy replied, not everything I had the honor of meeting some of the World War I pilots that came to the aircraft plant, I know their planes weren't as fast or maneuverable as these, but I would listen to everything they said, then I would apply it when I was flying like how to skid sideways so they can't get a clear shot at you in a straight forward flight, along with a lot of other tricks, Lieut. Harrison replied. If the American pilots could fly like that right out of school. Lord help any country that wanted to pick a fight with them Buddy got a smile on his face with a sense of pride, who knows how they are going to react in the heat of battle. It can be quite chaotic and sometimes confusing. Also, there are times when you do two or three flights a day, then fatigue sets in. That can be an enemy itself. The G forces do take a toll on a person's body with that Buddy asked the lieutenant if they could set up an area to work out the lieutenant said. Of course, I'll let you know where. With that, the flight leader Lt. Harrison headed back to the barracks area. Axle and some of the ground crew came over to refuel the planes, make them ready to go back up at a moments notice. Axle asked how did it handle Buddy replied I'm very happy with the plane. It handles like you said it would it's always good to talk to you about these things thanks for the heads up. Axle said if you want to know anything about flying you just have to ask me, he and Buddy both had a good laugh about that one As Buddy headed back toward the barracks area he reminisced about home wondering how his mother and Uncle Jim were doing. Buddy remembered the night his mother had returned home she had dated this man a couple of times it was a Friday night about 10 o'clock. He heard a car door slam. He looked out the window and saw his mother hurrying up to the house. She seemed to be distraught. The front door close, she went straight to her room, not knowing that he was watching he would sometimes sit in the dark just looking out the window. He wondered what was wrong with his mother as he walked by her door that was slightly ajar he could see her sitting on the bed with what looked like a shoebox with what appeared like a piece of red cloth. It looked like a scarf. He knocked on the door, causing Paula to quickly look up. She stuffed the cloth back in the box, closing the lid, asking him anxiously. What are you doing up this late. He said I couldn't sleep. I saw you come into the house and go straight to your room, you looked upset. Is everything okay? She replied as good as it can be just a bad date maybe someday when you're older you might understand. He could tell she was overcome with anger. Then she became quiet, a little more relaxed. He gave her a hug then returned to his room. He never wanted his mother to be upset or cry. He knew she had done so much for him plus sacrificed a lot, in the past he had asked who his father was. She would only say you may know in time, but he is dead, if the subject had been brought up when Jim was with them, they would look at each other with questions whether to tell him or not, that's the way they would leave it. Buddy would never push the issue. Because he knew it would upset his mother he always wished there was something he could do to make things better for her. One night, just before graduating from high school, he and Jim had been to a ballgame, Buddy said after the game can we stop and talk? Of course Jim agreed. So they stopped at a restaurant Buddy said to Jim, I'd like to know what happened, why my mothers like she is. He told his uncle what he had witnessed several times also about the shoebox with the red scarf. Jim turned his head away, not knowing how to tell his nephew what had happened, but he could not bring himself to lie to Buddy. Maybe it was time that he knew so Jim proceeded to tell Buddy in some detail of what happened that dreadful night in Canada also about the red scarf. After Jim was finished there were a few moments of quiet as his nephew tried to process this in his mind. Then he asked the question that Jim really did not want to answer, but knew he had to, Buddy's normal blue eyes turned steel gray; so am I the product of what happened that night? Jim choked with emotion, said yes, you are, there were several moments of complete silence. He asked Jim, what was the significance of the red scarf, He told Buddy the only thing I can figure is the guy that did this to her must have been wearing it. Somehow she got a hold of it and brought it home. Why, I don't know, I have also witnessed her coming home from a date doing the same thing you saw her do pick up the shoebox pull out the red scarf, sobbing and crying. I guess that's why she cannot have a normal life with a man. There sure have been plenty that have tried, but always ends up the same, now I hope this conversation never gets back to my sister. She would not want you to know these things, Buddy told Jim that will never happen, thank you for being honest with me.

Buddy's hatred for this person intensified the more he thought about it. Can you tell me anything more about this person, Jim said all I know about him is he was a pilot in the German army, His name was Wolfgang. Buddy told Jim he would do everything in his power to bring revenge to this vile person that did this to his mother. After the graduation ceremonies were over his mother was out with Jim and CT he came home to pack before going overseas Buddy got the shoebox out, then took the red scarf then put the box back. This would remind him every time he flew what his secret mission was and that was REVENGE. As Buddy came back to present reality he realized he was one step closer to his goal. Of coarse there were a lot of questions, was he still alive and where was he? Also was Buddy a good enough pilot to bring him down. Unknown to Buddy, his nemesis was closer than he thought also that they would eventually come face-to-face.

CHAPTER THREE

Briefing was at 0:600, the next morning Buddy was up much earlier he was ready when the other pilots came in the latrine, one of them said. Early bird gets the worm ah Buddy said the Sgt. Pilot, Buddy smiled nodding his head then headed for the mess hall he was thinking the system was different here than in the states they had Sgt. Pilots, in the states you had to be an officer. He liked the Sgt. Pilot a thin, wiry type of person named Sgt. Larry Whipple, known to everyone as Whip. He had a great sense of humor that was a great thing, especially among the pilots when you see a friend get shot down or another plane that belongs to us goes down in flames with no parachute come out.

Buddy went through the line then headed for the tables. He saw Maj. Morrison along with flight leader Lieut. Harrison. They motioned for him to sit down with them. They seem to be in somewhat of an intense conversation. The major said I hear you're quite a pilot, to that Buddy replied maybe, but I still have a lot to learn. I hope to do as well in actual combat. The major replied, that's when you're training will kick in. We've all been there, had the same questions no one can tell you how to react, you have to learn that on your own, but from what I understand from Lieut. Harrison your evasive maneuvers were extremely good also somewhat surprising of a pilot that just came out of flight school, Buddy went on to explain that he had been flying with his uncle before he ever went to flight school that seemed to help a lot. The major went on to explain its regulation that you have to be a wing man the first time you go up also it's normal to fly as a pair that helps protect each other, but sometimes you get separated that's just the way it is up there. Buddy replied that's fine by me, at least, I have somebody to point me in the right direction. They all had a little laugh about that one. The major said everything else would be covered in briefing with that all the rest of pilots filed out and into the briefing room.

The mission for today the major said is escorting the bombers as usual. Also, there will be a lot of enemy fighters in the area, so keep alert and your heads up do your best to protect the bombers also for the new pilots if you do go down and are captured, there is a strong cell of French resistance in the area. If you see someone cross their fingers, then give you quick nod, they would try to get word to help you get rescued if possible of course not everyone can be rescued unfortunately, but they do the best they can, with that they were dismissed then headed to the flight line to their individual planes. The ground crew was busy helping pilots get buckled in to their planes. Buddy was trying to remember the name of the guy that was helping him, the trouble was he had met so many men it was hard to remember their names but he remembered his face then he remembered his name was Nigel, as he finished with Buddy, Nigel tapped him on the shoulder, saying good luck and kick some you know what, then waited till Buddy fired up his plane gave him a thumbs up then climbed down off the plane, flight leader Harrison taxied out with Buddy beside him they all took off in pairs, climbing, heading for the channel just before heading into France they spotted the bombers then leveled off about 20,000 ft. altitude where the bombers would fly. As they maintained their flight he was still anticipating what it's going to be like they were a few hundred yards ahead of the bombers, he wasn't quite sure what to look for, but he was told, look for specs in the sky. Then suddenly he saw specks in the sky. At first you are not sure what you're seeing then a few seconds later, he was sure so he pulled up beside flight Lieut. Harrison and pointed at 12 O'clock high. The Lieut. shook his head yes. Buddy pulled back to his wing position. The Lieut. came over radio saying here they come ready or not, the specks grew larger and turned into fighter planes, Buddy wasn't sure if they were a Focke Wulf's known as FWs or Messerschmitt's known as Me's. Of course, it really didn't matter, shortly after that the Lieut., banked over and went after what looked like an ME as they got in range Lieut. opened up, bullets and tracers went past the enemy plane. The Lieut. was pulling to the left then the plane they were after was getting hit, the Lieut., kept firing the plane started smoking coming apart then rolled over headed for the ground, Buddy realized that was how it was done, the Lieut. said over the radio there is one off to your right go after him, Buddy accelerated banked over going after the enemy plane he was sure it was an Me, as he got closer he pulled the trigger felt his plane shudder as the guns started firing, he did a few short bursts the plane in front of him saw the traces go by, the plane started making some evasive maneuvers, Buddy stayed right with him, never letting up, firing more bursts from his guns. A little smoke started coming out of the front of the fuselage of the enemy plane. Those four 20 mm cannons started doing there job. Then he saw a few more tracers start hitting the Me. Buddy pulled the trigger again, the enemy plane started coming apart then headed for the ground. His first kill, he wondered when it ever came to that how he would feel, he was a little excited about it, but relatively calm he knew that was his greatest asset. Lieut. Harrison said over the radio good going, you got him, as did you Lieut. Buddy replied. They wasted no time going after two more Lieut. Harrison was in hot pursuit of an enemy plane, Buddy saw ahead of him one of our planes being chased by a German. So, Buddy took pursuit. It took him a few minutes to catch up to them. He wasn't sure, but he thought the enemy plane was after Whip, so every time they made a maneuver, Buddy would do a counter move to stay with them. He saw the enemy plane throwing some rounds at Whip's plane then Buddy was in position and squeezed off a few rounds. The tracers were right near the German's wing Buddy kicked his rudder hard pulled the trigger again hitting the enemy plane. It started smoking then took a nosedive heading for the ground as Buddy watched the plane took a hard right then headed away from the action still smoking, he thought about going after him then decided against it. The voice came over the radio said thanks mate. Then, someone yelled look out Yank you got somebody on your tail so Buddy started doing his evasive maneuvers he went into a couple rolls then a loop, leveled off skidded sideways did a couple more rolls the opposite way, skidded sideways the voice came over the radio again said good work yank you brushed him off. At this point, Buddy, had gained quite a bit of altitude, looking down, he saw an FW go after the lead bomber shooting the front of the bomber doing quite a bit of damage, It started a slow downwards spiral toward earth the FW swung back around and down drilling more shots into the bomber, even though it was going down he did this a couple times, this upset Buddy so he took after him. He was a few hundred yards away, so he pushed the throttle as far as he could to get as much speed as he could out of the Hurricane. It took him a few minutes to catch the plane. Buddy was surprised to see such a shiny plane he got close enough to start shooting at him. The rounds and tracers went past his canopy, then this plane that he was after started doing some wild maneuvers, Buddy pursued him, realizing real quick that this guy was a very good pilot also his plane was fast. The FW tried to make a loop to come over and behind Buddy, but CT had taught them about this, to be careful. So Buddy broke around , pulled up then back around like he was taught, suddenly came in behind the FW again, this time, somehow, he managed to get a little closer than before, Buddy preferred to get in closer for a shot instead of the usual 700 to 800 yards. He liked it around 300 to 400 yards. Something else CT had taught him your shots would be much more effective at this range, it can be dangerous. But that's a chance you take. Buddy took full advantage of being close then started firing. He knew some rounds hit the plane he was chasing when a puff of smoke came out of the front by the engine. He also saw some of the tracers hit their mark, there were more extreme maneuvers then started pulling away. His plane was faster Buddy realized he would never be able to catch him, about that time. Lieut. Harrison called over the radio to break off. Buddy wanted to pursue, but new it was useless to even try, the FW was going to out run him, after what this guy had done to that bomber crew he wanted to give him some of his own medicine but there'll be another day. So he broke off and headed back toward England. He was a little behind the other ones as he accelerated to catch up he noticed a plane kind of lagging behind the rest of them with some smoke coming out of the back, Buddy pulled up beside him and saw a big smile on Whip's face also he wiped his brow and shook his hand like he was sweating, Buddy had to shake his head, then chuckle, about that time Lieut. Harrison fell back to check if they were all right, they gave him a thumbs-up then Lieut. accelerated backup with the rest of the group. Before long everyone had landed as Buddy stepped out on the wing after shutting everything down. He looked around and saw Whip at the end of the runway off to one side the trucks there making sure there was no fire Buddy could see his friend on the ground walking around, he must be okay, they all headed for debriefing so they could compile their information, they wanted to know who saw what first and where the flight leader reported that his wing man was the first one to spot them from quite a distance pretty good eyesight? Asked the guy that was interviewing Buddy, of course, he tried to downplay it somewhat. I might've been in a better position or just lucky enough to spot them first. He went on to ask him other than the one kill, you went after another plane can you tell us about that one. Buddy went on to explain what he had observed also what the enemy plane had done, that's why he had gone after him, was there anything unusual about this plane, yes, Buddy said it was very shiny. There were moans and groans from the other pilots in the room. Somebody said the Wolf is back. He asked Buddy to tell more about the incident as he explained to the interrogator about some wild maneuvers this plane had done and how fast it was also that it started pulling away from him. He was sure that he had hit it a couple times. Also there was smoke coming out in the engine compartment. But before that, the plane he was after tried to double back around to get behind Buddy, he considered this pilot to be very good also unpredictable. After several more minutes of these questions he left the debriefing and headed for the mess hall. He remembered shortly after he stepped down from the plane his hands were shaking. He wondered what that was all about maybe it was from coming down off an adrenaline rush, he didn't know so then quickly dismissed this thought as he entered the mess hall collected his food saw Whip setting at a table with some other pilots so he joined them, he noticed that Whip's hand was bandaged Buddy asked him if he was okay he said of course with a big smile. The worst thing about it, the nurse that took care of me was a bit of a hag wouldn't you know if she had been a sweet girl. I would've liked some sympathy oh well, also it's hard to put this old bloke down it was just a scratch. Thanks mate for the help earlier, well Buddy said, I saw what you did to that German plane you were chasing, nice work so I couldn't let that go unnoticed, about that time Lieut. Harrison joined them after a few moments he said to Buddy, you are a hunter, when you see things you go after them and hunt them down, another pilot spoke up saying Yank, the way you went down after that German plane, reminded me of a hungry hawk swooping after it's pray. I agree, said Lieut. Harrison, but then you have another problem, you are going to be hunted by the Wolf. He will come after you because of what you did to him. So be wary. I might also say if other American pilots are trained and fly as good as you do coming out of flight school that's very good Buddy instantly felt a sense of pride, but then again, he felt he still had a lot to learn, about that time there was a commotion at the door. Everyone turned to look, then several men ran over to greet this person, there was plenty of pats on the shoulder and the arm several men acted like he wanted to shake his hand, but hesitated, Buddy could see from this distance that this person had quite a bit of disfigurement on his face and hands of what he could see it could've been fire or hot oil, maybe both. One of the biggest nightmares for a pilot is to be in a plane when it catches on fire or extremely hot oil gets on you, your hands and face, so once it touches you it's almost too late to do anything about it. Maj. Morrison escorted the pilot to the table where they were setting Lieut. Harrison smiled then stood up, grabbed the pilots arm, then introduced, Buddy This is Lieut. Bill Jackson, Bill this is Lieut. Buddy Williams from the US as you can tell, of course you know the rest of the chaps here. Bill pointed to Whip who had a big smile on his face, yes my comedian friend. I thought of you often during my rehabilitation. I may not be able to smile with my face but I can smile inside, Whip got a little emotional then came back with. I would've visited you more often but I had to be here to keep these blokes in line. You know, they would've all got in trouble without me here. They all had a good laugh about that one. The Major asked, how was Bemis? Bill replied, he didn't make it there was too much infection. The table got quiet for a minute with that. Bill sat down facing Buddy now my new friend. I heard you had an eventful day. If you remember nothing else, I am a product of Wolf's revenge. He doesn't forget he never waivers until he gets his revenge. I hear you are a hunter. I hope you fare better than I did. I am one of the lucky ones they tell me I'm alive. I've seen the Wolf follow a plane down and drill him into the ground for revenge. We also know he has more than one plane, when his plane gets hit and he has to take it down not far away, there's another one just like his he will turn right around come back up after you, anyone can always tell it's him, he's got the shiniest plane in the sky also the fastest. He makes sure about that, he lets you think you're chasing him then he will double back around then, he has you. I sure hope you're the man that can get him for men like me and some that didn't make it, if you ever get a chance to fly up next to him, you'll see a wolf painted on the side of his tail also a bunch of British insignias under his canopy, another pilot told his story of what he saw several other ones had stories, this went on for a while. The conversation slowed down a little bit then Buddy said I hate to break things up, but there are things I have to do as he stood up and told Bill good luck my friend. I will do my best to fulfill your wish. Bill replied. I'm sure you will with that Buddy turned and left the mess hall headed for the flight line he knew the crews were working on planes getting refueled and patched up in case they had to go again, before Buddy had left to go for debriefing he mentioned to Axle he felt the rudder was hanging up a little bit. As he approached he saw that they were working on his plane Axle said we were just finishing up, that they had found the problem with the cable for the rudder, we fixed it. Also, he said you got christened today the first time out, a few holes in the back of the plane. One of them had pinned the fuselage against the cable for your rudder, Buddy said yeah, I'm sure glad I had my head down, Axle said we heard what you did up there today we're proud of you the next time, give him one for us. Sometimes we get so involved in what were doing down here. We forget about what's going on up there, Axle said. Just remember, we're here to help you in any way we can, as he walked away to be with his crew that had finished up with their refueling then they got the call to go back up the pilots came out of the mess hall headed for the planes. The Lieut. had a quick meeting in front of the planes where they were informing them that radar had picked up some activity coming across the channel. It wasn't long before we had them fired up and back in the air. Not long after they had reached around 30,000 feet they spotted planes coming across the channel, someone yelled out Stukas, which was a fighter bomber the Germans used for dive bombing. Also there were a few fighters Lieut. Harrison saw right away what was going to happen. They were after our radar, he said over the radio. The Hawk with a few other men go after the dive bombers, the rest of us will take care of the fighters Buddy immediately banked over going after the dive bomber closest to him. It took him a few minutes also few rounds to get him, but then he had to pull out real fast because he was headed for the ground. The dive bombers can pull out easier their wings are made for it. Our fighters were able to take out a couple more but a few bombs were let loose he could see them hit the ground knocking out a couple buildings also one of the radars. They must have been planning something big they like to knock out the radar Buddy noticed some of fighters were going down in flames. He sure hoped they were German. As Buddy came back up, he spotted one of our fighters being chased by two German fighters. One of the enemy fighters was slightly to the side so Buddy headed straight at him he thought he recognized Lieut. Harrison's plane was the one being chased as he went by the lieutenants plane he opened fire at the on coming fighter. The enemy was firing back at him they were going head-to-head maybe luck was with Buddy, all of a sudden the enemy plane exploded Buddy banked off to miss the debris coming off the other plane, as he pulled back around he saw the Lieut. had out maneuvered the plane that was chasing him, looking around they saw that all the enemy planes were headed back across the channel. They brought their planes into land, they all headed for debriefing. Of course the ground crew came right back out refueling rearming them, ready to go back up after the debriefing, Buddy approached the Lieut., I would never question your orders, but out of curiosity he asked why did you send me after the bombers, the Lieut. replied you are a hunter you have that reputation now. I wanted those Stukas stopped at all possible. I knew they were going to go after the radar, which is one of our biggest assets because it alerts us early. Warning us also where they're coming from, they must be planning something, but I knew you would do everything possible to get them, that way we could concentrate on the fighters that were trying to protect them even though they did some damage I was told we still have radar in operation. I also appreciate you pulling one of those Nazi's off my back. To lighten things up a bit Lieut. Harrison smiling said how come you didn't take both of them off me. I know, Buddy replied. I'll have to talk to my mechanic about that I don't know if my rudder could handle it maybe it would be too much excitement for my plane. They both laughed, with that they both headed back to their barracks. Buddy felt good about the conversation he had with the Lieut. also, he was sure glad to see his bunk, after that last skirmish he felt a little tired. He woke up with a start, dreaming about being in a battle with Wolf of course, that would wake anybody up. Knowing there was going to be an early briefing today he decided to get started after eating, everyone headed for briefing. after the upper echelon received information of the attack on the radar. Also some information they got from intelligence that something big was about to happen. That's why they called the early briefing There was a little excitement here today the major called the briefing to attention in a loud voice, Introducing Capt. Harrison. He had got his promotion, which was long overdue the way the war was going things are sometimes a little slower coming. All the men in the debriefing hall give a big cheer the major said without further ado, we're sure we have a big job to do today, so I'm sending two sets of fighters up early and keep some in reserve on the ground, so Capt. Harrison with Lieut. James take your fighters up first. The other ones will stay on the ground ready to back them up.   Everyone filed out of briefing headed for there planes, Capt. Harrison told Buddy as they were walking toward the planes that once we level off you take the lead, your eyesight seems to be sharper than most. We want to take advantage of that, Buddy said Yes Sir with a smile on his face. The ground crew was making their final preps to the planes they were helping pilots get strapped in Nigel was helping Buddy then tapped him on the shoulder good hunting Buddy gave him the thumbs up as the captain pulled his plane out Buddy and the rest of them followed suit. They took off in pairs. Dawn was just breaking as they got airborne. They climbed to 20,000 feet in a circling pattern over the channel. Not long after the second circle daylight was approaching fast. As they circled they were climbing in altitude. They wanted to get as high as they could, about then Buddy spotted the specks some were large some small, indicating bombers and fighters, Buddy couldn't believe his eyes, because these spots seem to cover the whole horizon. He throttled back to where the captain was, in motion with his hands he covering the whole sky back and forth. He also indicated large dots along with small dots, the Capt. nodded his head. Then he pulled his plane forward dipping his wings numerous times this meant to everybody else there were a lot of enemy planes in front of them. By now the planes on the ground had been notified by radar of large concentration of planes coming across the channel. They were airborne to fortify the planes that were already up there. The ground crew was scrambling around repairing planes trying to get them in the air. They had pilots on standby for the disabled planes. It was going to be an all-out effort. Whip had accelerated up beside Buddy looking over shaking his head. It wasn't long before both sides were involved in individual battles the Captain, Whip and Buddy were after some Me's Buddy went after his enemy plane. It didn't take him too long to shoot his tail off. It just headed for the ground smoking. He looked over at Whip, who had just annihilated the plane he was after he had lost sight of the Capt. Buddy was in a position to come down after some bombers. He was able to pick out one on the way down. As he came back up he was able to get another one, there were so many of them. It was almost like shooting fish in a barrel. Everywhere you looked there were enemy planes. He was much more interested in knocking out the bomber's as were a lot of our fighters. Everyone knew they were headed for London to do as much damage as they could. By now the smoke was really thick in the air, planes were getting hit everywhere no matter where you looked planes were going down bombers and fighters as he went after another bomber, then Buddy felt a couple of thuds he knew he'd been hit someone yelled out lookout Yank someone's right on your tail, some of the guys still called him Yank instead of Hawk. Of course, it didn't matter if someone's on your tail what they call you. Buddy, without even thinking, skidded his plane sideways suddenly backed off the throttle, the plane overshot him and accelerated pulled back on the stick as he came up, got the plane from underneath and obliterated him. Then he pulled up beside a plane looking over saw it was a FW, the pilot was a young German his eyes were wide open from fear. It almost looked like he was sweating, sometimes you forget, there are real people flying the planes it's not just nuts, bolts and metal, but that's what it was all about man against man plane against plane nerve against nerve. Buddy for some reason, when something like this was going on his calm nature kicked in maybe that's why he was such a good pilot if you get rattled you might make a mistake then the enemy has you, also being calm is easier said than done, again that's when you're training kicks in it's critical. Also how well you take your training. Buddy saw two ME's ahead of him about that time a plane pulled up beside him, it was the Capt. They both pointed at the enemy fighters in front of them, they went in pursuit, as Buddy closed in on the one he was after, he threw some rounds at him the tracers went by his canopy he immediately went into some evasive maneuvers, Buddy stayed right with him throwing more bullets at him. He hadn't witnessed this kind of maneuver since he chased that shiny plane. This went on for a few more minutes. It seemed like longer but it wasn't, Buddy got a couple more rounds off, but he was using a little caution. He didn't know how much ammo he had left. This is one time he didn't want to run out. Then he heard someone yell lookout Hawk. That shiny plane is after you; Buddy gave another burst of rounds at the plane in front of him. Then he saw smoke coming out of the engine compartment. He really wanted this plane but Wolf was on his tail, so he figured I better try to get out of there he new if it was Wolf 's plane then he would not be able to out run him. However, he might be able to out maneuver Wolf. He also realized he was probably too far away from anyone that could help him, so he banked off away from the plane he was chasing. He saw tracers go by. He thought he felt some of them hit his plane, he wasn't sure, so he started pushing his plane doing barrel rolls, kicking the plane sideways went in a tight circle did more rolls his plane seemed to be working just fine. All the time Buddy was doing his maneuvers. He somehow felt he couldn't get rid of. Wolf, as he leveled out skidding sideways more tracers went by his canopy, over the radio someone yelled he's still there, it sounded like Whip, I don't think I can get there to help you. Not long after that, Capt. Harrison announced for everyone in our group to break it off, Buddy knew they were all running low on fuel. He felt like he was in somewhat of a predicament. Also, those G forces he was doing with the maneuvers he was making were taken a toll on his body. He was glad his adrenaline had taken over. Low on fuel, knowing Wolf's plane was faster than his Buddy realized he had one shot left one last maneuver up his sleeve, either he ran out of fuel, possibly get shot down by Wolf or do this one last extreme maneuver very few pilots would ever attempt this. He had no choice. He automatically pushed the throttled as far as it would go, pulling the stick back as far as it would go, climbing straight up watching his altimeter, then push stick forward, going into an outward curve hurtling toward the Earth. Somebody yelled out, I don't believe it the Yank is doing an outside loop. Several Spitfires from another squadron heard what was going on with Buddy and the Wolf; they broke off to come over to see if they could help. Wolf would never back away from a fight, but he had just been out flown by the Yank. He didn't know how to handle this, he never thought that the person flying that plane doing the loop would finish it, figuring he would break off early then Wolf would have him in his sights. This didn't happen. Now he wanted this Yank, more than ever. He had first shot at him on an earlier flight, then this time he shot at his best friend Hans Kessler caused him to go down to land with his plane smoking, now he had done this. It was really humiliating Wolf never questioned his flying abilities. Although he did question the fact if he had to, would he have done that maneuver, yet he had never been put in that position. On his way back to the base he wondered how his friend Hans was. Wolf was replaying that flight over and over in his mind, he sure wanted another day another time another chance at that Yank they call the Hawk. Going after the bombers unknowingly had taken Buddies group across the channel into France. Sometimes, you're concentrating so much on what you're doing you lose perspective of where you are. His group really didn't want only Buddy left behind, any one of them would have relished the idea of staying back to help if they could, however, they were all low on fuel, Buddy was concerned about his own fuel running low so he opted to throttle back to just above cruising speed. He could see the channel well, so he lowered his altitude. Also he felt the blood finally coming back into his legs and his hands from the G forces. Then his heart jumped up in his throat as three planes pulled up beside him. He was sure glad they were Spitfires. These were the fellows that came over to help when they heard over the radio the commotion about Buddy and Wolf, one of the chaps came over the radio saying to Buddy. Nice work what you did to that dingo, which is what Australian call a wild scavenger dog. That outside Loop an all, you've got more guts than most We're glad you took up the cause, volunteered to come over to lend a hand with more pilots like you it will make a difference. We appreciate the help, especially with that dingo, but we would use a bit of caution, the pilot went on to say, I bet that sent him back with his tail between his legs. Buddy had to smile about that remark. This was his first encounter with Australians. They were also a great bunch of chaps, as they pulled away from Buddy, one of them radioed back. How are you doing on petrol mate? He replied, I'm a little past empty with that they throttled back to stay with him. They weren't going to let anything happened to him after the day he had just gone through. Finally, Buddy came in sight of the base where he was stationed so he gave them a thumb's up and replied over the radio. Thanks for the ride back. So the three planes banked off and headed for their base. As Buddy landed, his plane started to sputter, but there was still enough fuel or petrol as they called it, to taxi toward his normally parking place, but the last couple yards he was sure he had to coast in, he was glad he didn't have to circle the field, his last words to himself as he shut the plane off was; thank you Hurricane for bringing me through, with shaky hands and shaky legs. He wondered if he could stand out on the wing. After he stood up for a few seconds just standing there he was able to step out on the wing he looked down to his amazement a loud cheer came up from the crowd they had barely landed and had all got out of their planes when they saw Buddy come in, so they gathered around his plane to give him a welcome back for what he had done to their favorite hated German pilot. The captain said, I hate to break up the celebration, but we all have to go to debriefing, so with moans and groans from the other pilots they headed toward the buildings. This break had gave Buddy a few more minutes to get the energy back in his legs enough to get down off the plane just as Axel with some of the ground crew gathered around, Axle said, I understand you just brought my plane back from an outside Loop. I don't know any pilot that tried that and returned. As Axle turn to walk away he turned back he said we heard what you did to Wolf today, Buddy replied how many people knew about this, Axle replied, just about everybody in Britain. I guess there were about 200 planes in the air. As a matter of fact, they pumped the chatter over the radio so all of us could hear. Buddy just shook his head. Then he said to Axle the information you gave me about the hurricane was invaluable, today it held together, I remember what you said, to never give up on it. I may not have been

able to outrun the Wolf but I sure as hell out flew him today. Normally Buddy wouldn't boast about these kind of things but he did today, giving the plane its dues, with that he turned, heading for debriefing where of course, there was a flurry of excitement about how many planes there were, also how many went down, which were mostly German bombers and fighters sadly enough, some of our fighters, along with theirs. Interrogation was about the same as usual. But they wanted to know more about the German plane that Buddy had hit with smoke coming out of it. They wanted to know if there were any unusual marks on it, his remark to that was the plane had banked to one side. He saw a few rows of British insignias under the canopy also a bear on the tail, then one of the interrogators spoke up, that was Hans Kessler, that is Wolf's longtime best friend, you are sure adding up a column of numbers first, going after Wolf sending him smoking then his best friend smoking, today you out fly him with an amazing outside Loop. The only good thing about this is he will be coming after you with a vengeance, leaving most everyone else alone. I'm just wondering what he said at his debriefing that might've been interesting to hear.
After several more questions Buddy headed to the mess hall. He was hungry. There were quite a few well-wishers; congratulations also a few "amazing feat", mate. As he made he's way through the line, Whip walked up behind him, saying, look at the extra helpings he's getting, I'm sticking close to you, their feeding you extra good today. Maybe some of that will fall on my tray they both had a laugh, about that.

CHAPTER FOUR

After exercising the next morning to loosen up from the pounding he put his body through the day before, Buddy ended up at the mess hall. He got his tray went through the line, headed for the table where Major Morrison, Captain Harrison and Whip were sitting with other pilots. Buddy sat down. The major said I would've loved to have seen the look on Wolf face when you did that Loop yesterday. I'm sure there were a lot of people, even amongst his own ranks that would've enjoyed seeing that, of course, no one in his ranks would've made any comment about it. They wouldn't dare, but I wonder what was being said behind his back, I would have given anything to hear what Wolf said to his interrogator, if he said anything at all. The major asked do all American pilots trained to do what you did? No Buddy said I don't think so. It was my choice. I asked my instructor CT, what the most extreme maneuvers he thought there was to get out of a situation like I was in at that time. A lot has to do with your altitude. Also if you trust your instruments one of the pilots asked, how do you know when to do something like that, Buddy replied. I don't know. It's just something that I do. I try to figure out everything but then it seems like I automatically do things. Lucky for me that the things I have done so far worked out for me there is something that comes over me. I am almost calm when I do these things. I guess that might be in my favor. I sure don't claim to be the best pilot as I said before I still have a lot to learn. One of the other pilots said maybe its time you started teaching us some things. Everyone seemed to get a chuckle out of that. Buddy was getting a little nervous about all this. He didn't care to be in the limelight or be somebody's hero that was the last thing he wanted. He tried to change the subject then was glad when it was time to go for briefing.

The briefing was similar to yesterday's several flights would go up earlier, leaving the rest of them to come up later. It really worked out good the day before. Of course they knew the Germans would be more prepared this time, but we were to go ahead with the same plan again. So Capt. Harrison, Lieut. James with the rest of you that went up yesterday early, repeat that again today. The Germans took a great loss yesterday we sure took a toll on their bombers hopefully we will keep doing that. Sadly enough, we lost a few of our planes. Today's flight was not much different from the day before. There was an extreme amount of bombers it seemed like a constant barrage of our fighters knocking down their bombers. Our planes against their planes day after day this seemed to go on for some time. One day, in the midst of the battle Buddy pulled up along side another fighter looking over he realized it was German also very shiny a German fighter with a lot of British insignias under the canopy. So there he was looking straight at Wolf. Buddy raised his fist with his index finger pointing and his thumb up, cocked like a gun, pointing it at Wolf and motioned like he was shooting at him. Wolf was a bit dumb founded to think anyone would have the gall to mock him. This had to be that arrogant American they call the Yank or Hawk. Wolf also saw the star on his uniform shoulder. He also knew most pilots would have turned away from him trying get away. He immediately rolled over banking around as hard as his plane would go trying to get behind that Yank, Buddy thought about following him, but he knew his plane wasn't as fast so Buddy did just the opposite going the other way hoping to get behind him, but by the time they leveled out. Wolf realized there were a lot of planes between them. He would bide his time, but eventually he would have his chance to do justice. Wolf was amazed at the tenacity of this young pilot it almost reminded him what he was like years ago. Buddy realized suddenly that his plane was real low on petrol, the Capt. called out to brake off he hated to do this in the thick of battle, but he headed back to the base for refueling Wolf remembered when he was younger how his mother was so very domineering while his father was meek, mild. He worked as a machinist in a factory. Wolf would go with his father quite often where he worked Wolf learned a lot about machinery with some tricks of the trade. He learned how to brake machinery down then put it back together. His father was a very good machinist. It's too bad he had no backbone when it came to things at home. His father drank quite a bit he would stop for a few drinks on his way home from work quite often, probably to take the sting out of his life. Wolf never truly respected his father he could not respect a man that let a woman belittle him with every opportunity available. With her domineering nature and her smothering attitude toward Wolf he vowed to never be weak, to make his needs first in life. He developed his own sadistic ways, when he was just a young boy he would torment any small animal or young child that showed any sign of weakness. He was also very mean about it. His mother gave him the name of Wolfgang to give him strength. She would not accept him being weak like his father. He took every opportunity to prove his strength, always being physically fit. Also enjoyed showing off his strength and physical prowess, he would challenge all of the schoolyard boys, no matter if they were younger or older, or anyone dared to challenge him he would always find a way to defeat them, even if it meant fighting dirty if he thought he was about to lose the fight. He reminded himself what his mother was like then gather the meanness also the strength to win the fight. There were times when the children's parents would appear at their door to complain to his mother what he had done to their child. She would always come to his defense, and would make short work of them. Unlike his father who would not get involved, even though he knew what his son was like with the depth of the meanness he was capable of. He remembered seeing what Wolf had done to some of those poor animals. Instead, he would head to the local bar to drink and drink, it would never solve anything, but it would take the sting out of her onslaught also his son's depraved demeanor. As the years went by Wolf grew very tall, with his blue eyes, blonde hair, high IQ, along with his incredible strength, the girls that knew him admired his outward appearance. Then there were times when they would find him repulsive. Wolf would only associate with young people of his caliber, which were very few. Upon reaching a very young adulthood he had managed to involve himself in several offensive situations with young girls, having been called in to the principals office where there were accusations of sexual cruelty, even some of the local authorities were called in, of course, his mother would always come to his defense, that the parents of the young girls were at fault for not teaching their girls better. It was never his fault. As far as she was concerned, those nasty young girls taunted him, asking for what they got. After these incidents he would be boisterous and brag about this to anyone that would listen by now his list of so-called friends grew even smaller. One day Wolf was approach by one of his teachers to join an exclusive group of young people for the betterment of Germany. The teacher explained that this group would take up the majority of his time. He would have to live on a campus also emerge himself in the culture and the programs for this group. Wolf was extremely excited about the prospects that this teacher was suggesting it took him a minute or so to absorb everything he asked the man how soon, will this be arranged, I will know by tomorrow he replied. If you are sincere, Wolf said, I'm definitely sincere, then thinking I can get out from under my mother's thumb also with her constant barrage of insults to his shamefully weak father. He was beside himself with anticipation he could hardly contain himself. The next day he was informed of a meeting that afternoon. Of course, he was accepted. Almost giddy with excitement he rushed home informing his parents of his decision, his mother was dead set against this she did not want to lose control of him, again his father had little to say about it maybe it was for the best he thought, remembering well he recently showing a little gumption he took Wolf to the backyard to whip him with a stick for something that his father was outraged about, because one of his friends that he drank with had a young daughter that had been brutally assaulted by Wolf. However his father came out a lot worse then he did in fact his father had to go and have stitches in several places. The bad part about it was Wolf's laughing at him when it was over. Yes, maybe they could teach him some respect. Within a few days everything was all set his teacher had made all the arrangements for him to be enrolled in the organization. He returned home from school early that day, informing his parents that it was time for him to leave. Also he would not be able to come home for the first time in her life. His mother fell silent. She waddled over and picked up something turned back handed it to Wolf, a handmade Scarlett Scarf. It was unique in color and the way the tassels were designed. She said almost tearfully all I ask is for you to wear this to remember me Wolf looked at his mother, then at the scarf as you wish. With that he went to his room to pack his clothes, thinking to himself that he would wear this scarf not as a memory of her, but as a constant reminder of his life up to this point. There was no sympathy for his parents they deserve each other. Grabbing his bag he walked back into the room where they were completely ignoring his father, who was still bearing the scars that Wolf had given him in their one and only confrontation in a small way, he almost had respect for his dad for his futile attempt to correct him, that young girl should never have taunted him with her innocence. He took pleasure in what he had done. Then there was a knock at the door Wolf answered it invited the man in to the room. He excused himself for a moment, going into his room. She recognized him as a government man she knew he was one of the teachers placed in the school by the government to spot potential candidates for the military, they said it was for the betterment of Germany. She turned to say something to him, but by the cold stare in his eyes she would not be able to dominate this man or be able to change his attitude towards her son. Wolf entered the room he noticed a deathly quietness, his teacher saying, let's go with little emotion do you want a moment with your parents before we leave? I'll wait outside, Wolf replied coldly, definitely not. With that they left there was a strange silence between himself and the teacher on their way to his new life. It was several hours away by train then a short distance to the compound Wolf settled in rather fast, falling into a daily routine. It may not have been as comfortable as it was at home, but he preferred this 100 times over living at home Wolf learned quickly what was expected of him. This was a military school, loyalty was the most important attribute expected from everyone, the instructors would test the candidates from time to time, he would always pass easily, he had no trouble making friends, most of his classmates were of the same mentally, he became very good friends with his roommate, Hans Kessler he was a very large man, with a quietness about him. Of course Wolf, being just the opposite they seem to complement each other. They would often be partners in class studies they also spent a lot of their recreational time together. Hans was an older student he really helped Wolf to achieve what was expected of him. Hans was well respected among other students also his teachers Wolf excelled both physically and mentally. He was above most of the students. However, he still had his mean streak. If anyone of them showed weakness he would exploit that in every way he could. Hans being more advanced was able to help him advance of course Wolf would always be boisterous about his accomplishments, he secretly wanted to do better than Hans, he would secretly applaud himself if he did do better than his friend, but that was seldom actually he enjoyed that kind of competition. He knew that to compete against somebody better than you, then able to beat them it was twice as rewarding. Of course, he would take every shortcut possible to accomplish this then silently gloat. Unknown to Hans or Wolfgang, they were being surveyed more than the other students because of their superior intellect also physical abilities. There were always a little bit of rivalry between the two. Of course Hans was advanced in certain things, because of his age and experience. However, Wolf did excel in his own right. They would test each other, which would help to make them keep each other sharp.Time past by relatively fast days turned into months, months turned into years Wolf liked his life here he never looked back. Wolf grew into adulthood rather fast. His mother did manage to come to visit him. She was proud to see that he was wearing the scarf she always took pride in and mention it to his disdain. Hans had a completely different childhood, his family being poor farmers. They always had food but had to struggle for clothing and shoes, just simple things. It was especially hard in the winter time to obtain heavy coats or hats to ward off the freezing cold. He was no stranger to hard physical work with long hours working in the fields from before dawn to after dark. It was a simple but good life with no frills at all.He and Wolf on occasions would receive privileges so they would visit local taverns, where there were always women eager to meet young men. It was clear from the first time the two men had contact with the women Wolf's appetite for women became quite different then his friend Wolf preferred much younger women there were times when he would leave the tavern by himself only to return with one or two young girls. It was doubtful if they were even old enough to be there. He would ply them with drinks they would be much easier to take advantage of. Hans on the other hand, preferred much more mature women he did not care for this dark side of Wolf, it was also obvious that he would get what he wanted one way or the other, even if he had to force the issue. Very seldom, was he seen with the same young girl. On occasion the local police had to visit the compound with questions about one of their students. Several times he was reprimanded for his actions, but that never seemed to stop him, Hans made excuses not to go with his friend anymore. He immersed himself in his schooling because he had applied for officer's school it wasn't long before he was accepted. This left Wolf behind. Of course, knowing it would not be long before he would follow to become an officer himself. There was no doubt about that. Hans was relieved in away to go on without him. He liked his friend but did not care for his actions as to the way he treated women. Several years went by until Wolf was accepted to officer's school. Again he excelled in his classes. It wasn't too long before he achieved this status as well, once he graduated and became an officer He made a special effort to find his friend. Wolf was overjoyed to see Hans also to catch up with everything that had happened while they were apart. Wolf asked his friend what he was involved in, Hans replied. I've been thinking about you lately. I would like to show you something. They headed to a large building. As they entered Wolf came to a complete stop staring in amazement at this shiny thing with wings, Hans went on to tell his friend. They were using this particular machine for reconnaissance. Wolf said I had heard about these, so do they really fly like they say, Hans replied, they sure do. Would you like to see, Wolf jumped at the chance with that his friend started to yell out orders to his men. They quickly jumped to, they made the plane ready for take off as they approach the plane they put on some flight suits, leather caps and goggles Wolf's eyes lit up his emotions were wild. Hans asked, are you up for this; Wolf replied wild horses couldn't drag me away. So with the help of the crew the plane fired up Wolf was amazed, he could hardly breathe. The crew opened the doors Hans revved the engine, the plane moved out of the building. As he pushed the throttle forward, the plane started picking up speed slightly bouncing across the field as it picked up speed. Before long they were actually in the air, climbing in to the sky Wolf could not believe what was happening, he had never felt this way in his whole life, they kept climbing higher breaking through the clouds. It was a beautiful day, especially up here then Hans started doing some maneuvers then headed for the ground. He pointed at the ground to show Wolf, what to look for, also in front of Hans was a machine gun as they approached the ground. Hans reached over flipped off a safety then started firing at some targets that had been set up. He circled a few times firing at the targets until there was nothing left but shreds. They continued to fly for while making more maneuvers then headed back toward the area where they had taken off, he throttled back slowly and brought the plane in to land not far from the building they were in before. He was actually able to swing the machine around in front of the building. He was shutting the engine down while the crew was busy pushing the plane backwards into the building. Wolf was excited beyond belief. As soon as he got out of the plane he went straight to the front looking at the propeller wondering why there were no holes in it, he asked his friend how do you control that, Hans said a man called Fokker designed a gear that was driven by the propeller shaft, it will only fire when the propeller is in the opposite position, no matter how fast the propeller turns or you fire the gun, it doesn't matter, when you pulled the trigger it will miss the propeller every time. Wolf never smiled. Except for now when he had a large smile on his face while shaking his head in disbelief, trying to absorb all this information in such short amount of time. He said to Hans what do you mean you were thinking about me? Do you think I could be a pilot? It did not take much persuasion or encouragement to get Wolf flying he became one of the best pilots, of course having the advantage of knowing machinery that he learned working with his father he had an advantage understanding the workings of engines, as well as the mechanical end of an airplane. Not only could he fly, but he could help with the maintenance and improvements. He was a quick study and excelled in this early field of aviation. Wolf, remembering his first combat flight after practicing a few times with Hans or any other pilot that happen to go up. Of course this being different because it was for real. It was hard to contain his excitement. But he knew he had to concentrate often wondering what it would be like the next thing he knew he was right in the middle of it, Wolf's plane being superior to those he was against. He went right after them being quite successful on his first encounter he was higher than the plane he was going after, so he swung down behind the enemy plane immediately start firing his excitement level was higher than expected as he continued after the plane that did some maneuvers to try to evade his attack, but Wolf stayed right on him continuing his assault. As the plane he was after started smoking and headed strait toward the ground. He kept in pursuit, shooting all the time until he was only a few hundred feet from the ground. Then he broke off, and immediately started to accelerate he could not wait to get to his next target. It was not long until he had his sights on another plane. This time he followed that plane down continuing to fire until it crashed. He accelerated heading back up then realized the battle was over somewhat disappointed he scanned the sky for any sign of a plane he could have a confrontation with but there wasn't any. So he headed back toward the base. As he landed the plane he quickly jumped out and noticed that Hans was also landing, who had also had several victorious battles as they walked away from their planes. Wolf could not contain himself as he recapped everything that happened point after point. Hans relayed to his friend, after you see that you have done sufficient damage to the plane you're after and it's going down. It's time to break off save your ammo and your fuel for another battle. Sometimes it's hard to calculate how much ammo you have left. However Hans had a feeling that his advice was falling on deaf ears. Then he had a grim thought perhaps I have created a monster. Several years had past they had been in many battles. Some they had won then sometimes they ended up on the ground smoking themselves. Wolf had been wounded a few times it seemed like he enjoyed this. Also he was proud to show his scars with bragging rights if his plane had damage enough to bring it down for repairs he expected the ground crew to be ready. Also if he was wounded he wanted to be able to have his plane patched up along with himself then return so he could fight more if the battle was still going on. Look out if the ground crew wasn't working fast enough. He would shove them out of the way to fix the plane himself then he would go back up with blood mixed with grease on his hands or arms. He was definitely fanatical, but rest assured, he added up his scores, they were definitely higher than anyone else along with this, he acquired rank with privileges, his superiors, were very proud of him. He became a leader, but also was feared by most of his fellow men. Although proud of his wounds and scars. He was particularly vengeful of anyone that dared fire on him or cause him or his plane any damage. During these years he still maintained his vengeance against women. He had many occasions with young women, his cruelty towards them seemed to increase with his scars and accomplishments. They were great bragging rights. He certainly took advantage of these, on several occasions he had been confronted by a father, brother, or friend of the girls he had accosted had tried to face Wolf but to no avail. He always maintained his physical prowess. He had amazing durable strength and would subdue them quickly, ferociously. This also gave him more encouragement to brag. Hans and Wolf had remained friends although Hans would not associate with him when they went to town. He did not want Wolf's reputation off the base to extend to him, but on the other hand going in to battle with his friend alongside of him was some what of a comfort knowing if he got in trouble Wolf would be the first person to help him. There was still a bond of sorts between them. Wolf was wounded towards the end of this war. He was forced to take some time off while he was recuperating German intelligence paid him a visit asking him if he would be willing to do some espionage work for them he agreed immediately

So after some training along with learning how to speak English. He found himself in Canada and was quite taken back by their way of life. Enjoying the nightlife also the women then again younger ones he also seem to have a knack for getting information. There were several times he went across the border into United States being amazed at such thing as a production line. This consisted of household items, cars, amongst other things in great quantities. He was highly interested in what kind of aircraft they were producing. Also, what the capabilities were to compare them with the aircraft that his country was producing there was a certain amount of German underground in both countries which helped him tremendously with information about innovations and technology always comparing them with his country, collecting this Information to take back with him some time in the future. Canada was quite industrious in its own right. Wolf fell quickly in step with the nightlife spending money. He always seemed to be popular, but his evil streak continued. He remembered one incident very well. There was young girl that worked at the hotel. Very pretty, kind of shy the type he was certainly attracted to. He always had a feeling that they were taunting him with their innocence and their beauty. He felt he had made himself available to her several times. She seemed to ignore his presence. He vowed he would somehow have his way with her one way or another, he would accomplish his goal, the more a young girl would evade him the more challenging it was to have them, one evening he approached her asked her to have a drink with him. Surprisingly, she accepted this was encouraging to Wolf. However, after one drink along with some conversation of course mostly about him with how good of a pilot he was he invited her to his room for more drinks. She quickly refused and seemed to lose interest. This foiled his attempt to have his way with her in his room. However, on his drives through the country at times he had observed her walking, presumably to where she lived. He imagined on some farm that is all there

was out in that area. He realized shortly after the refusal she had disappeared. Knowing this was about the time she would leave. He drove the automobile he had borrowed from before and went looking, then finding her on her way home. He got out the car quickly grabbed her throwing her to the ground then pulled at her clothing and swiftly brutally with no remorse, took her innocence. He was being extremely cruel with her because she had evaded him for so long, denying him his selfish pleasures. What he couldn't understand was why any female could resist him and deny him what he wanted. After all, he was a well decorated very good-looking rather arrogant person. How could any female resist.
The next day the hotel owner got wind of what had happened asking him to leave. Also, some of the authorities were informed about this, Wolf was asked to leave the country immediately while he was packing he remembered there was something missing it was the one and only Scarlet Scarf that his mother had made for him. He remembered he had taken it with him when he went after the girl down that road, but there was nothing he could do about it now.

    Upon returning to Germany a lot of things had changed. He was very upset because other countries had got together and forced them to give up a lot of their military equipment, along with all other projects for the betterment of Germany, there were still some secret sects of the military that were working undercover with their most vile projects like bombs, explosives also military type planes that were being developed behind the backs of the allies that were against them, that had made the rules forbidding them to do just exactly what they were doing in secret, but no one seemed to have the ability to investigate or stop them.

About this time in history, along came a young man with radical ideas about the direction Germany should be taking. Wolf thought to himself, this man could become powerful in time. He seemed to have the ability to rile people with the speeches so Wolf decided to join an organization called the Brown Coat's also known by other names. After becoming a member, which was a personal guard for this person, who slowly but surely built the war machine. However Wolf still loved his flying. Germany went to war with other countries like Belgium, Poland. Also, Russia, then they marched into France. They were able to take a lot of French countryside of course this set them up close to the English Channel with the idea of eventually taking over England at some time. However, one big obstacle was in their path that was the English Channel. He could not get his tanks, armament, heavy equipment or whatever else he needed to invade across that body of water. Germany had produced several good fighter planes one was the Messerschmitt or Me. The other was the one he preferred called the Focke Wulf or FW, the British had their fighters. The two most popular of their planes one being the Hurricane, the other a bit more popular is called a Spit Fire a little faster also more maneuverable then the Hurricane. It didn't matter a whole lot, but it's good to know your opponent's weakness and abilities Wolf remembered his first time back in a plane it was The FW he couldn't believe the difference in the power and maneuverability compared to the planes of World War I it was unbelievable.

When World War II broke out Germany's new leader gave his loyal officers, most of the high-ranking positions, especially the ones that had done work for him in the past Hans and Wolf were among the chosen ones that showed their loyalties more than once to their new leader.

During some down time Wolf had a visit from his mother telling him that his father had died. Also that she was left to fend for herself. Wolf showed little to no emotions concerning her plight. She did leave a package for him, it contained another scarf exactly like the one she had given him years before. Somehow she had found out that he wasn't wearing the scarf she had given him before maybe he had lost it. After she left he put the scarf on feeling the same revulsion as before, from his childhood. A few months later he was informed that his mother had passed away there was no feeling of sadness with Wolf. Only bitter contempt he was glad that part of his life was over.

Wolf snapped back to reality from his reminiscing, he quickly checked his planes gauges then refocused on the task at hand his opponent that he had just faced. Thinking he had been facing a more seasoned pilot especially since he'd preformed that outside loop also being able to maneuver the plane he was flying to get close enough to shoot hitting him also his friend Hans then being arrogant enough to do that ridiculous thing with his finger and thumb like he was shooting a gun at him. No one can do that then get away with it. He was going to make sure of that also the punishment would be extra harsh.

CHAPTER FIVE

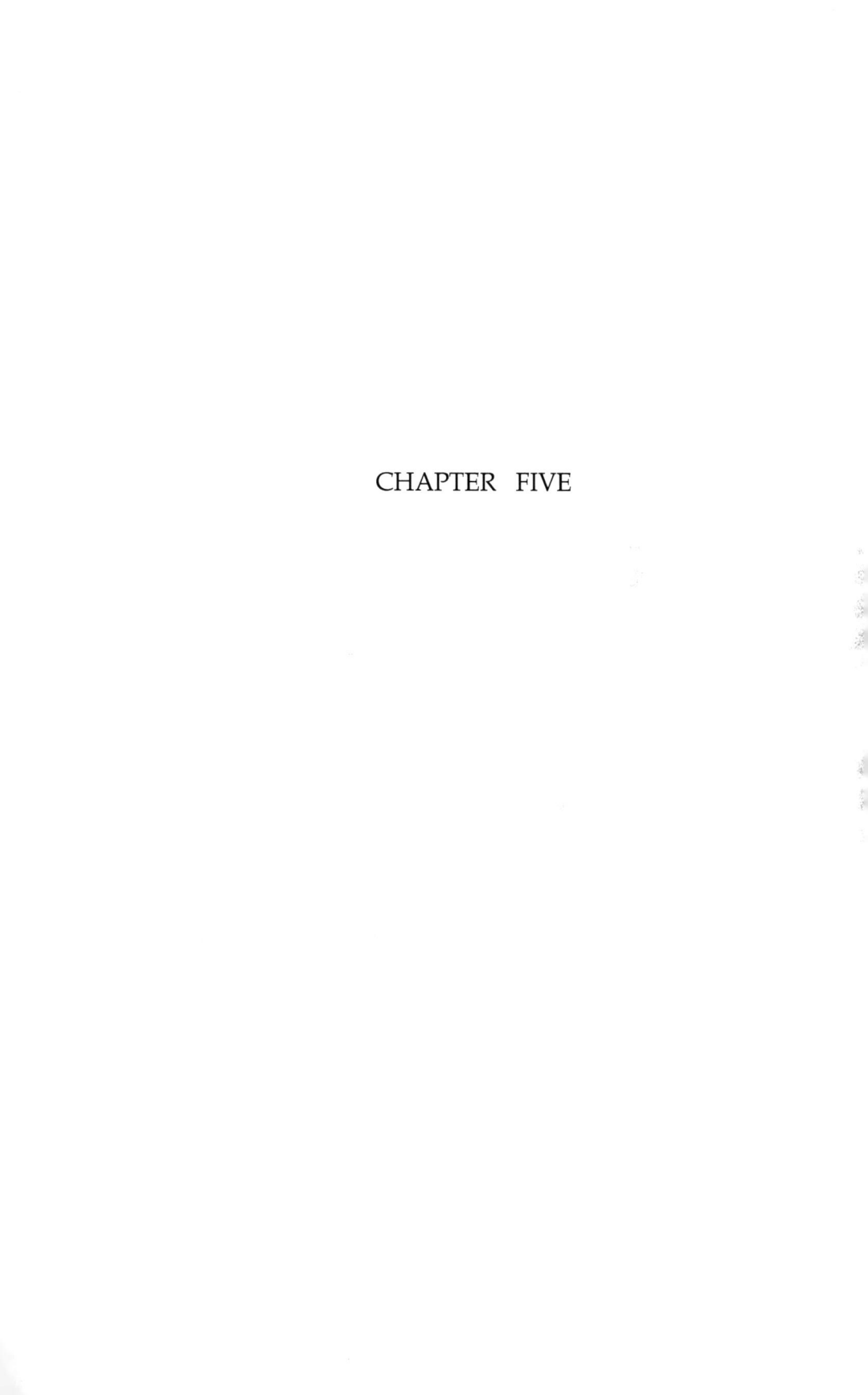

Buddy was late getting to the mess hall that morning he was in a makeshift gym, working out. They were ordered to stand down today because of the weather. It was a good time to do some much needed repairs also upgrades on the planes. He had come up with some innovations that he and his uncle had been conversing about through the mail Axle had received these updates having his men apply these to the planes with very good results. Of course, Buddy was right in there with Axle up to his elbows, the crew chief would chuckle to himself amazed that this officer would be doing this. There was a time when he had grease on the end of his nose. They would laugh together. Later Buddy took time out to clean up to go eat. There was kind of a eerie silence when he entered the mess hall as he passed through the line he noticed a silence among the men, some of them would not even look him in the eye a couple of men shook their heads and gave somewhat of a weak hesitant kind of smile as Buddy walked to the table he saw the Major along with Whip and several other men. Whip had hardly touched his food. The other men were laying there utensils down as he approached the table and sat down. Buddy looked around noticing everyone in the building was very quiet normally there was a lot of activity men talking, joking, but there was none of that, what did everyone lose their best friend, Buddy asked? Whip managed a weak smile also had kind of a glossy look in his eyes almost like he was ready to cry. Maj. Morrison cleared his throat, Buddy. I have something to tell you, I know by looking at you with your easy way you have not heard the news, we have just received over the wire that Pearl Harbor has been bombed by the Japanese. This is true and factual, it has been confirmed. They have sunk most of the battleships along with a lot of other ships. There are unknown amount of dead and unaccounted for. Evidently, there was no prior notice of this. It was kind of a sneak attack, Buddy sat in silence for about 5 min. pondering a lot of unanswerable questions. He realized that's why everyone was so quiet. He got up quietly leaving the mess hall. His normal quiet demeanor was turning into rage his mind kept going over and over about the conversation that had taken place. It was hard to understand how anything like this could happen and why. If anything anybody would've thought this would have come from this side of the world because of our help with the English. Buddy ended up at the small gym they had made doing his routine with more vigor than usual. The makeshift gym was taking the brunt of his beating. Nothing seemed to calm his rage, so he decided the best thing to do was run, he felt the cold December air nipping at his face. This only added to the intensity of the run he had no idea what the time it was when he started. He just knew he had to run and run the hours went by every once in a while Axle or one of the ground crew would look out and see him running, lapping the airfield many times. He lost all track of time. Finally he felt his energy draining away from him. It felt good he only hoped it would last he wanted no energy, he only wished he could drain his emotions as well, exhausted he headed for the showers. He turned the water on as hard and hot as he could stand it almost scalding him. Maybe he was trying to punish himself, but he didn't know why. After he was done he headed for his bunk area as he approach he saw Whip leaving the area as he looked against the wall. The guys had hung an American flag he did not know where they had found it, but he felt a great sense of gratitude. He turned to Whip and the other men, with a nod. Whip knew that his friend would be okay, or at least as good as he could be under the circumstances. Everyone respected and gave him his space. Sleeping rather fitful through the night, having several dreams mostly things he did not want to think about. As he woke the next morning, the first thing he saw was the flag he laid there for a few minutes. Just taking it all in, hoping it for a bad dream, but knowing it wasn't. Looking down at the corner of the flag there was a long piece of paper attached to it. As he looked closer he saw it was signed by everyone in the squadron, including mechanics, officers, everybody, Buddy got emotional and silently thanked everyone. He knew he hadn't offended anybody the day before the way he acted. He just needed to blow off some anger everybody understood that as he got up to start moving around. It seemed like every muscle in his body was aching from the punishment he put it through the day before. He showered quickly with hot water again to loosen up his muscles as he left the building. He realized it was another cold, gray, overcast December day, just like the day before. Heading into the mess hall he noticed a lot more commotion and noise Buddy was grateful for that as he sat down to eat. He turned to the captain saying I like to talk with you later if it's possible, flight leader Harrison said definitely, after eating he rose to his feet and with a very loud voice. I want to thank all of you, looking at Whip nodding for your generous gesture, I salute you one and all. I am very proud and honored to have been accepted to help serve this country. You are all brave and fight the good fight. You have been fighting for a long time, also have not wavered. You have stopped a maniac in Germany. Your families are being bombed your country being bombed in your own back yards I can't imagine what it would be like. My heart goes out to you your country and your families. There's no doubt in my mind now we will be involved in war up to our neck's here and over there. I know our production lines will change from household products to war machines, planes along with other necessary equipment to fight with. Some people think we don't have the stomach for fighting, but I know the president will declare war also Congress will back him up on this one. You will see in a few months that it will take us to get back on our feet then start rolling. What the Japanese did to us with this sneak attack woke up our nation then there will be a terrible resolve against them like they have never seen it will come down on them like rain. Nobody does this to America and gets away with it we will not roll over and take it, I promise that. Buddy was silent for a minute then turned to the Major the Captain along with everyone else saying thanks for letting me get this off my chest. I appreciate it. With that Buddy turned then walked out heading for the gym to work out when he was done with his work out. He went out to the flight line. The crew chief and his men were working on the planes. The weather was cold Axle looked up to see Buddy, he decided a nod would be sufficient, it was about that time the Captain came by checking on the planes to see how the ground crew was coming along also to check with whatever Buddy wanted to talk about. Capt. Harrison started the conversation, I know if you really feel like you need to go back to the states. Maybe join the fighting against the Japanese, we would all understand. Buddy replied, I would like to go fight the Japanese right now for what happened but I do have unfinished business here. That's why I wanted to talk to you. I know the weather's been bad, but there's got to be something I could do I really need to fly I need to do something no matter how dangerous or what it entails the Capt. said , I will put my feelers out to see what I can come up with. It may take me a day or so, but I'll do what I can, Buddy confided in the Capt. saying, it seems like things are all clogged up in my mind maybe this will help me. It was late the next day when the Captain caught up with Buddy he said I have something you asked for. Tomorrow you will be transported about 50 miles from here you will find out the details when you get there. Buddy said thank you very much I need this. The next day he was transported to another base. He was told to report to Capt. Roger Mudd. Upon arrival, that's just exactly what he did. The captain greeted Buddy with a welcome to our base I will take you to where you're going in a minute. I know you've heard it all, but our hearts go out to everyone affected and involved in Pearl Harbor. That's enough said. Buddy replied I appreciate that they left the building got into a vehicle and was transported to a hangar number seven, after a few minutes they arrived at the door of the hangar, there was a guard of course this was classified a secret mission, so they had to show their identification. Once inside the building

Buddy got excited. Setting there in front of him were three planes, known as a Mosquito, also called a wooded wonder twin engine plane used for bombing or a fighter, sometimes reconnaissance while the Capt. and Lieut. Were looking over the plane they were approached by five other men. They were all introduced to each other the one Lieut., introducing himself as Dean Hunter. He was an American navigator or pilot. Lieut. Hunter remarked they couldn't have picked a better pilot than you. They had recognized each other, Buddy remembered that Dean had studied to become a pilot, but he preferred navigation over flying as they shook hands, looking at each other, knowing nothing had to be said about Pearl Harbor, Buddy said with a light smile well if I fall asleep or decide to just jump out for cup of coffee someplace at least there will be someone to fly and navigate the plane Dean replied if you jump out for some coffee. I'll go with you, I get a bit tired of tea there was a bit of a chuckle. Likewise they couldn't have picked a better navigator. The Capt. gathered all of the men together explaining these planes have all been modified to carry bombs. If you decide to accept this mission you will be flying into German territory. There'll probably be heavy flak in some areas also you will be flying at night mostly. There was no doubt he would take the assignment no matter what the circumstances. At this point, the Capt. asked before I go any further I would like to make sure everyone is on board with this? They all agreed they were on board. Good, your final briefing will be this evening before you leave. You're all dismissed everyone snapped to attention, saying yes sir. With that, they all filed out of the hangar talking to each other about things, but not about the mission. They were transported a short distance to a building specially designed to house pilots and crew when they were going on a special mission. It was a type of barracks away from the main base. They didn't want anyone talking about their mission, which they wouldn't. They all ate and rested for the upcoming flight. That evening they were transported back to the hangar.

Capt. Mudd showed them on the map where there were headed. So the navigators could plot this mission, you're going to bomb a Nazi stronghold, not too far from a large city. It was an area set up for top German officers to party and blow off some steam. It was about dusk, when they opened the doors. Three planes started their engines taxied to the runway. They got their clearance to take off. It wasn't long before there were airborne. By the time they got across the English Channel. It was dark. They were to head across France then into Germany. Buddy was really impressed with this airplane. He could feel the power with this twin engine wooden wonder. It sure didn't feel like something made out of lumber. He hadn't had the chance to do much maneuvering. It was just a matter of take off then pointing the plane in the general direction of Germany with Dean's help, but just by the feel of this plane it would probably handle extremely well, the other two planes were following close, we had made arrangements before taking off to do some clicking over the radio to make sure they were together, it was a very dark night just a sliver of moon, which made it hard for anybody on the ground to spot them right now they were about 20,000 feet, of course they had the latest mobile radar, and navigational equipment. So once they were on the way. It was just a matter of sitting there letting the planes do the job. Buddy had lots of time to think and sort things out. Maybe quell some of his rage back into common sense, he had no idea how much time had passed. It seemed like hours. There had been several incidents where they heard flak behind them. Also they had picked up a few blips on the radar of course they had strict orders to avoid any confrontation with anything on the ground or in the air if at all possible. More time passed finally Dean said we are not far from the target. Suddenly, the night was lit up with powerful floodlights and then all hell broke loose, flak everywhere. Dean had taken control of the plane, bomb-bay doors were opened. Then Buddy could feel the plane lift, as the bombs were dropped.

He immediately took over control of the plane banked an accelerated then pulled the stick back climbing, altitude would be their only friend, the ground lit up as the bombs hit. According to the radar all of the bombs hit their targets as all three planes lit up the flak got even worse. They were throwing everything they could at us. Sadly enough, the plane behind him to the right took a hit and came apart with a loud pop. At least they had dropped their bombs before they were hit. They were trying to climb out of there when he heard something hit the plane but he wasn't sure about the damage. Everything seemed to be okay he checked the gauges they seem to be okay, but the plane did shudder quite a bit, Dean was able to see the silhouette of their other plane occasionally when the flak lit up the sky in that area. However now he had lost sight of the other plane because he was so busy checking their own plane, he was hoping they had not been hit too bad as they continued to climb heading south, a bit different pattern than the way they came hoping to avoid some of the flak, then Dean mentioned that he was picking up some enemy aircraft on radar. That is one thing they didn't need right now. However, a blip on his radar had lit up for a minute because of their planes in the air Buddy pushed the throttle all the way forward. The plane gained speed right now. He was glad to have that extra power. He was sure he could basically outrun any enemy planes out there right now also it was still dark so they wouldn't be able to visually see them. They weren't far from French soil. Then, out of nowhere they ran into more flak, Buddy felt a big thud by the right engine. It started to cough smoke was pouring out what he could see, so he feathered that engine right away then shut it down. It was better to do that then let it catch on fire, then thought to himself this is not good they still have a long way to go. He did not know how far they could fly on one engine. Dean asked him how they were doing Buddy replied, hang in there we lost one engine as you can tell I don't know how far one engine will take us hopefully it will hang in there. One thing is for sure, it will slow us down a lot we're okay now until daylight. Dean said we are in French countryside now, but it's quite a ways to the channel can you see the other plane he asked Dean, I thought I saw him back there a while back, but I'm not sure if he's still with us. I haven't seen any explosion with luck, he is still flying. They flew like this for quite a while. Slowly they were inching across the French countryside but time was still against them. Any minute now, they would start seeing glimpse of daylight, of course, they would be sitting ducks for any hungry German plane in the area knowing what they had just done to their high-ranking officers. He thought to himself wouldn't it have been great if that top ranking official, that maniac leader of Germany at the present, would have been in that compound and was blown up with the rest of them, but I guess we can't ask for miracles, the other miracle we could ask for now would be to make it across the channel. By now they had made a good amount of distance across France, then noticing his gauges, Buddy realized the temperature was slowly creeping up that would mean the oil pressure would start slowly dropping. That would not be good for them. Now the other enemy against them was starting to appear and that was daylight, along with that would be more chances of enemy planes also being spotted from the ground. All this was stacked against them. Plus, the engine that was running was still climbing into the dangerous area of heat, with the low oil pressure, he may have been pushing the engine a little too hard the only advantage they had was altitude when they were being pounded by flak he took the plane as high as he could go with it, now is the time to cut back the throttle let the engine cool while losing altitude, so they were okay again for a while. He was watching the instruments, checking them every few seconds. This went on a few times the temperature went up, the oil pressure went down he had to put it in a dive, the engine with gas open it would start again as it did a cloud of smoke came out the exhaust, Buddy wasn't sure how long he could keep doing this without the engine failing. He didn't want that to happen. He wanted to land the plane under power, and not have to dead stick in with no engine. A few more minutes of flying would take them closer to the channel still hoping to make it. He asked Dean how far it was now, about 200 miles Dean replied, Buddy knew he had to do something and soon he got on the radio asking is anybody out there, but there was only silence on the radio yet on it again, calling out if anyone was out there, then something did come over the radio. It was kind of broken up, Buddy was sure it was the other plane that he had made it through. He was sure glad about that. Just then the engine coughed, he realized this was it he had decided to sit it down while he kept the engine running. He saw a farmhouse in the distance there was a field very near, he was able to bring it down now. Heading in the direction of the farmhouse hopefully he was friendly, Buddy made his approach, bringing it down. It was hard to adjust the speed with only one engine, trying to keep it straight as it touched down. It got fairly bumpy he was able to keep it right side up. They both knew what they had to do the very second the plane stopped. They had to set the igniter to destroy the plane with the latest radar along with the bombsite and equipment. He brought the plane to a complete stop. They were able to exit the plane quickly Dean had set the igniter so they only had seconds to move away from the plane. Then there was a loud pop the plane blew up destroying everything inside, it was kind of sad Buddy thought it was such a great plane then again it had to be done. We did not want our equipment to fall into enemy hands. As they headed quickly toward the farmhouse, several men came after them from different directions. They were definitely German soldiers well armed. He and Dean had made it really close to the house. A very large man was watching everything from the outside of the house, Buddy looked over at this man dressed like a farmer, a Frenchman, probably that owned this farm while the soldiers were stripping them of their weapons, busy checking them out. The farmer gave a quick nod reaching up as though he was going scratch his head he gave the signal. As the soldiers continued their search of the two men, Buddy made eye contact with a young, dark-haired, pretty girl for a few seconds, presumably the farmer's daughter. She immediately turned, going into the house. Dean looked at the plane that was fully engulfed in flames. The two men looked at each other relieved that their plane and equipment was totally destroyed, gave them some comfort knowing that there was nothing to salvage. The soldiers put the two of them in the back of a truck then down a long winding road for about 20 min. When they came upon an area that was double fenced with several buildings inside and outside the fence. They were taken into one of the buildings outside the fenced area. Both were searched again separated then questioned for hours. They had been taught. If captured, name, rank and serial number which had nothing to do with what their mission was, both were very tightlipped about that. Also denying any knowledge of what had happened deep in German territory the night before. As far they were concerned they were on a completely separate mission, they were just flying along when one of their engines caught on fire forcing them down by the farm where they landed. After extensive questioning they were pushed and shoved to the compound area inside the double fence which was the holding area. A lot of men were there to greet them as they entered the area they were quickly escorted into one of the buildings to where there was an officer. British Major Adams who seemed to be in charge also a pilot, he probably led a group of bombers. Also there was a captain Tanner. They both introduced themselves. When Buddy introduced himself then his call sign the Hawk also known as the Yank there was a flurry of excitement throughout the building. The word had spread amongst the prisoners about this young American pilot along with his reputation. Of course, some the stories about him had been blown out of proportion, which often happens with stories. It was somewhat hard for some of the men to understand how he had even been shot down. But then Buddy relayed how he had been hit by flak, just before entering French territory. It was also hard for them to understand how he had brought his plane this far on one motor, he didn't want to say too much because you never know who might be listening, however all of this really lifted the spirits of the men. As Buddy looked around, realizing how deplorable the conditions were, in these barracks. The dingy lighting, cold a lot of men were poorly bandaged, men were coughing some of them had very deep coughs. They looked thin and pale you realize right away they were not being fed very well also they had makeshift crutches the bandages were falling off. Buddy tried not to make it obvious that he was checking them out. He was sure they were not looking for sympathy. They just wanted to hear something good about how close was it to the end of the war so they could go home and get a good meal. We all hope soon he told them. Dean was saying the same things, realizing these men wanted to hear something positive anything to lift their spirits. Buddy asked the major if he could walk with him outside he agreed. As he left the barracks Buddy said I know I can trust you because Dean verified it so I can tell you when we were captured by a farmhouse. This Frenchman gave me the sign. Major Adams said that's very interesting, then he informed him that the French resistance was working real hard to get the pilots out and back across the channel, he also told Buddy don't be surprised if somebody starts tapping on you in the middle of the night that will be a signal for you to move fast. I will take charge of letting the people know about the situation you had just told me. About then there was some racket going on at the front gate, it sounded like a bell ringing, then everyone in the barracks started filing out The major informed him it was time for what they called food. I will talk to you later. I need to take care of this. Buddy was in no hurry he wanted to observe. After most of the men had gone through the line Buddy filed in behind Dean quietly informing him of the conversation he had with the major when the two of them came to the table with the food. It consisted of a pot of some kind broth with a small piece of potato then was handed a very stale piece of bread. Realizing why the men looked like they did if this is all they had to eat. You could complain, but it would probably fall on deaf ears. What they were getting was barely enough to sustain you, their thinking was you wouldn't have enough strength to try to escape even if you did, how far would you get. Buddy took some time to think about the situation he was in, actually a prisoner of war wondering what the outcome would be. Suddenly, he felt a calmness come over him where it came from he didn't know. It just comes over like a warm blanket.

Buddy and Dean were shown to the bunks, where they would be staying. One side of the barracks was for officers and the other side was for enlisted men .Quite a few men were in the barracks, bomber pilots, copilots, fighter pilots navigators, gunners, engineers, ground troops. Rank was still observed officers and enlisted even Sgt pilots were with the enlisted men, being an officer had responsibilities, even in a prison camp.

Later Buddy approached Dean saying, well, I kind of got us in a mess here didn't I. Dean replied, you have to be kidding, remember this was a volunteer mission on both our parts. Also I don't know anybody that could have done what you did. Actually I was hoping that we wouldn't make it until after daylight and then had it out with that shiny German plane then we could've done one of those outside loops like you did before. That would've been a little more fun than what we did. They both had a little laugh. Seriously, Dean said I have flown a lot of missions with a lot of pilot's I don't know anyone who could have flown with one engine that many miles, you think about it. We could've gone down in Germany. We almost made it to the channel, I'd much rather be here, this close to England than where we were when we got hit.

A couple of men approached the two asking them to come over to their side of the barracks to talk for a few minutes as they approached the other men they all wanted to know the latest news of the war. After chatting with them for a period of time it seemed to lift their spirits. One of the men spoke up to Buddy wanting to know what it was like doing that maneuver to evade that German pilot by the name of Wolf. They wanted to hear the story first hand. So he proceeded telling them point for point just how it happened and how he was able to do the outside loop, luck was with him or I would have been splattered all over the ground. The men were trying to explain that it was great to have him here in person, telling them this story wishing this would all have been under better circumstances not here in prison. But then, this is reality. It was good to see the expression on the faces of these men, for a moment they were transported out of there to a much more pleasant environment, Buddy certainly did not want to be any kind of a hero, but by telling his story made life a little easier here. Even the weakest man with their bandages and all were given a boost. Of course, he would tell the story several times. Some one replied. I would've liked to have seen the look on his face when you did that, you actually were able to out fly him. While Buddy was telling his stories he was using his hands to show how planes would chase each other he had a very captive audience. Sadly, one of the men had been lying down on his bed propped up with some kind of pillow watching every move he had almost an uncontrollable deep rattling cough, but had a big smile on his face when Buddy was done with his stories and using his hands. He looked at the man. He wasn't coughing anymore. He had a blank stare in his eyes but the man still had a smile on his face. Someone picked up a blanket and covered his face. That brought things to a quiet end.

The front doors to the barracks flew open. Two guards stepped inside the door then to each side. They had what looked like submachine guns. Then a fairly tall image was in the doorway. Behind him were two other images. All of them poised to shoot anyone who attempted anything. The tall image entered into the barracks. He was definitely an officer maybe a Col, most likely S.S. in a flight suite. He ambled around looking at different people. The other two soldiers had stepped inside the building also, the officer said in a very loud voice. I am WOLF, there was silence in the building for a few seconds, then came some moans and groans in different parts of the room, he said with a sneer. You people are pathetic I want some information, he said, in somewhat broken English I'll get it one way or another. He started walking around the room slowly then stopped in front of the major saying I suppose you are in charge of this shabby bunch. The major replied yes I am. Wolf said I will deal with you later, as he turned to leave. He turned back toward the major. I thought your country would've give up by now. They're about as worthless as you people are in this camp on your knees, we will finish you off whenever it pleases us, then he turned back continued looking at the prisoners, mostly officers. Let's make this easy Wolf said, "I'm looking for an American pilot" with that, he took hold of one of the officers and pulled him to his face very sharply. The major jump to help the officer, one of the guards came right up to the major put the muzzle of the gun to his head gave him an order [what amounted to] back off, in German. Wolf said loudly again, who is the American pilot. I want to know now the officer just stared at him a little nervous. Wolf released the man then step up to another prisoner announcing the same thing. They would not divulge who the American pilot was. He said I will take you out one by one and shoot you, until someone will tell me who he is with that last comment Buddy stepped forward looking right into Wolf's eyes, saying, I am the American pilot walking straight to him. The guard tried to get between them facing

Buddy with his weapon you need these guards to fight your battles he said to Wolf. I guess you need them all around you to protect your hide. Wolf immediately shoved the guard out of the way now they were face-to-face, eye-to-eye. Maybe, just maybe, Buddy might have been a half inch taller. He glared into Wolf's eyes never flinching. Wolf said you are more pathetic than the rest of these people. You think the British are your friends and they care about you. Your people are dumb enough to think that your friends can win this war with your help. We will not only annihilate them then use their country and soldiers to destroy yours. Buddy's blood started to run cold. He would like nothing better than to tear into him right here right now, however the guards would not allow that to happen they would make short work of him with their guns.

    Wolf continued, saying, so you're the smart one, shooting down our planes, then got lucky shooting at me. Then my friend, along with that trick you pulled to get away from me that time I had you, suddenly Buddy got a smile on his face. Just knowing what had just been admitted. This made Wolf mad to think he would smile like this having removed his hat. It was almost uncanny the resemblance of these two men face-to-face. Everyone took a deep breath. Someone said, "what the." They couldn't believe what they were seeing; as they looked at both of them. They had matching red scarves. Wolf had a moment, with a strange look in his eyes almost of recognition, but of course this could not be. Buddy never wavered with his stare he was still savoring the smile that thoroughly upset Wolf. Although deep inside of him something started churning a question he had been asking himself about this person in front of him for quite some time. The name "Wolf' was this just his call sign or was it short for "Wolfgang" he would deal with this later. Right now he felt a revulsion building deep inside of him questions running wild in his head

Wolf saying I was in Canada for a while and visited your country. Yes, you have very good production lines using it for cars and household products. That's just the way you people are you would rather pamper yourselves then to get involved in war, the Japanese proved you have no stomach for war at Pearl Harbor with one strike, they wiped out all your battleships destroyed a lot of your planes, your country did nothing about it. Your war machines are made of paper. Also, your nerves for fighting are made of paper. Buddy's blood turned very hot, he raised his fist pointed his finger like a pistol and said quietly, pop, pop your dead. Wolf went into a rage, dropped his hat pulled out his Lugar jacked a round in the chamber put the gun to Buddy's head. Just then, the major jumped in and said you better not do this. Then there was a loud voice from the front door way a large rather pudgy person that hadn't missed any meals, was the commandant of the prison camp. Yelling Col. Wolfgang then went on saying something in German probably not to do this in my prison camp. Wolf stood there with a gun pointed to Buddy's head for several tense minutes. His finger still on the trigger looking slightly but significantly upward with his eyes meeting Buddy's eyes his finger tightening slightly on the trigger an even louder yell from the front door. He stepped back, putting his weapon back in its holster, with rage on his face turned to walk away, Buddy said as he reached down picked up Wolf's hat handing it to him saying, you better put this on your head. We wouldn't want you to catch cold. Maybe get sick and die before I have another chance at you up there. Wolf went to turn back toward Buddy but the guards stepped between them again, this time facing Wolf, by the order of the commandant. Wolf said in a loud voice, enjoy yourselves here for soon you will be transported to Germany then we will have our way with you once we have accomplished this so trust me when I say, it won't be pleasant. With that he turned and left the building abruptly. The commandant along with the guards left the building with the door slamming behind them. Out front you could hear loud voices shouting nobody quite knew what they were saying, but everyone was quite sure it was an argument between the commandant and Wolf.

Back inside the building there were a few seconds of silence then a big sigh of relief. Several of the prisoners were looking at Buddy. They had great respect for him after what he had just done, to stand up to Wolf like that. However, the question still remained. Even Dean remarked the resemblance is uncanny. Do you have distant relatives somewhere in Germany, sadly enough a lot of us do have family members in our past that lived there. Buddy replied not that I know of. As he walked away headed for the bathroom hoping there was no one in there. He felt something boiling up inside him. He had to be alone right now. Realization was apparently taken over his reasoning. He knew now, with no doubt he had been facing his archenemy, the man that had done those evil things to his mother and nobody knows how many other innocent women he had accosted, how many lives has he destroyed. The rage was building inside of him, almost like when he heard about Pearl Harbor. But this was a lot different this was aimed a little closer, actually right at him directly.

    Buddy wanted to run as he did in the past, he walked straight out of the bathroom to the major asking his permission to run outside, the major granted his request, so he quickly grabbed his jacket headed outside and began to run inside the perimeter of the fence. The guards kept a watchful eye on him. After a few times around inside the fence area they were not too concerned about him. They were talking amongst themselves about what the interest was in all the commotion concerning some prisoner. It was something the guards could talk about to relieve the boredom of maintaining prisoners. Of course, this was better than being thrust to the front lines.

Buddy maintained his running for quite some time, then realizing his weakened condition from lack of good food was taking a toll also draining him, which could be a good thing. He felt the best thing that could happen was to be able to drain him then again he wished somehow, someway, he could drain off his emotions. He didn't know if that would ever happen.

      There was nothing Wolf could do about this; the commandant had the right to stop anything from happening. Angry and frustrated he had no choice but get in the truck that had brought him and they headed back to his plane, on the way he was thinking about the American pilot going over what had happened, something was tugging at his memory besides the incident there were something he couldn't quite put his finger on it, but it was something he saw, the scarf kept drawing his attention. Why? He didn't know. Also his physical appearance the resemblance of the two was remarkable, but no one could be as striking as he was, as he kind of chuckled to himself. No one was as good-looking as he was. By now, Wolf had reached his plane, so he quit thinking and just concentrating on firing up his plane and taking off. There was a lot to think about later. One thing he knew he was glad they had him under guard. He also had a small amount of respect for the way the Yank had stood up to him. No one else would dare. Hans was the only person he knew that he respected or even looked up to. Reaching his plane, he was soon airborne looking for a fight with anybody. He would surely like to destroy something or someone today. Too bad the Yank is in prison Wolf would like to have a fight with him right now plane to plane guns to guns kill or be killed. He was thinking as he headed back to the base. Maybe he would just settle for a bottle of cognac.

Buddy was fairly exhausted as headed back in his barracks to where his bunk was. He had gained his composure back unwrapped the scarlet scarf from his neck, wiped his face and sat down looking at the scarf. It reminded him of why he was here. Also, this answered the questions, he was alive, he is here, but was he a good enough pilot to bring Wolf down, only time will answer this final question. Buddy never would brag about how good he was as a pilot, not even to himself. The one thing he did know was if he had the right plane at the right time. He would be able to go toe to toe with Wolf, now more than ever. He just wanted the chance. Today was one of the biggest pieces of the puzzle he had witnessed. With that he lay down in his bunk, no one would bother him tonight. Waking the next morning thinking that was the best night's sleep he had experienced in a long time. His head was clear he knew his agenda, things had really fell in place now all he had to do was get out of there and back to his plane, of course, he said to himself. That's easier said than done. As he got up from his cot, then stretched, looked around. There were a few guys already up. They were milling around, talking to each other. Buddy went outside it was very cold that morning like most this time of year. He did a couple of exercises to loosen himself up from yesterday. Then he went back into the barracks to his bunk area. Everyone was up that could get up by now even Dean. Buddy noticed that the men from the other barracks were there, getting the latest information, mostly about what had happened the previous day. Good morning Buddy said in a somewhat firm voice. Every one repeated good morning back to him kind of a surprise in their voices saying how Buddy was this morning. Compared to what had happened yesterday, almost like nothing had happened. Several of the men, including the major started talking to him about the incident that happened the day before, Maj. Adams said you either have to be the bravest person I've ever known, or the most insane, perhaps a bit of both The Maj. continued, you must know who he is also his reputation. He also mentioned you fired off a few shots and hit his plane along with his friend, also hitting him. Then you did that thing. How did you do that again? Buddy smiled then brought up his fist with his finger pointing and his thumb up like a hammer made a mock gun then said bang, bang. Or something like that Maj. Adams, shaking his head in somewhat disbelief at the same time knowing everything was true, smiling he said I've never seen anything like that and probably never will again as long as I live, but it was worth everything to see the expression on Wolf's face. You could tell he could not understand how anybody can stand up to him like you did, I must say it was a tense moment or two when he pulled out that Lugar and put a round in the chamber. I don't know if he would have actually pulled the trigger, but I wasn't taking any chances for once. Also, I'm glad the commandant showed up when he did. The Maj. started laughing along with everyone else even some of the men that were very sick and hurting. It did, Buddy's heart good to hear that much laughter. After several minutes the laughter died down. The Maj. With a smile on his face said loudly, "roll call" this was just a matter of discipline and pride a daily procedure also to show the Germans. They still had a sense of routine. Buddy looking around suddenly realized that most of the men from the other barracks had been there to hear all this they also joined in the laughter. Everyone filed out except for the ones that could not even move. Some of the men that were on makeshift crutches hobble out and marched around the compound, today, they had somewhat of a spring in their step. They knew also that the commandant would be watching them out of his window. He probably had just finishing his enormous breakfast. He was looking for a weakness in the ranks, especially after yesterday, but all he could see was men marching, hobbling dragging a leg, arms and legs bandaged heads held high, even some with smiles on their faces. The commandant didn't quite know what to make of it, was there going to be a prison break. This would surely make them happy. With a large belch, thinking to himself, he must remember to inform the guards to cut the prisoners portions of food down even more his theory, no food no strength. No escape. So the routine went day in day out with the weak broth, less potatoes than before. Smaller pieces of stale bread twice a day, marching around the compound, time went by. Buddy did exercise. He did start to feel weak, but did not give up exercising if no more than to warm-up his muscles. Never knowing when you might need them. Especially if Wolf showed up again and have to show him that gun again. One night, having a restless, fitful sleep Buddy noticed the front door open as images come in watching them approach Maj. Adams bunk first, then two other men. Surprisingly they came to tap on Buddy. He instantly got excited wonder if this was what they were talking about. Whispering quietly to go to the back of the building as he and several men, including the Maj. followed. They slipped out through some loose boards into the dark night. Buddy estimated there were about 10 of them. He sure hoped one of them was Dean. They quietly slipped away from the building to the fence, slipped under one part of the fence then through a small hole in the other one then a few yards to a wooded area. The excitement was mounting in all of them. They proceeded through the woods for quite a distance still being quiet as possible. Then they came to a small clearing on a narrow dirt road. There was what looked like a covered German military type truck with the engine running that they all climbed into. Buddy, got a little nervous along with some of the other men when the last two men getting in were dressed like German guards carrying submachine guns, thinking they may be taking them someplace to be executed, but Maj. Adams set their minds at ease by telling them this was the best cover anyone can get. If they were stopped, it would look like some prisoners being taken to another site.

Instead, after bouncing down this very long dirt road what seemed like it was forever they came to a rather large clearing. As the truck turned off the engine, and they all cleared out of the truck there was total complete silence. You could actually hear somebody breathing. Then the men started talking, finding out who each other was the Major introduce some of the men to each other. He was still in charge, there was little to no light except for the moon. As time went by, quietness descended on them, then somewhere in the distance there was a noise that sounded like a vehicle approaching. It had dimmed lights in the silhouette. You could tell it was another truck similar to the one they had arrived in. The men that were dressed in German uniforms with their weapons ready slowly approached this vehicle then it flashed its lights a certain way. Everybody seemed to relax a bit they were not real German soldiers as everything became quiet again, they all heard another type of noise someone said that sounds like airplane engines. The excitement started running through their minds, along with questions and prayers. Buddy noticed a couple of men made a cross someone else spoke up saying, could you do a couple of those for me. I probably needed more than you do. You couldn't tell if anyone was smiling or not. The noise became louder and more distinct. It was definitely the engines of a plane, as it drew closer it starting to circle one of the men by the truck flashed his lights twice then once, then twice again, like the truck had done, as it had approached this area, giving the signal it was okay to land with the moon shining bright. Also, with the truck, having its lights on kind of lit up this somewhat long clearing the plane made its approach skinning the tops of the trees bring it down then landing taxiing toward their end of the field swung the plane around engines still running. Then the door on the back of the plane flew open with a step dropping down close to the ground. The men about 20 of them, that were waiting moved quickly in to the plane filing in on both sides sitting down, buckling their belts.

While the steps were pulled in the door was being closed. Then the engines revved as it lurch forward heading for take off. Within 5 min it seemed from the time they entered the plane then it was in the air headed for the channel and England. The men that accomplished these missions were called the moon squadron. This is all they did was go out on rescue missions at night of course. These nights were lit up brightly with the moon. They are probably trained differently to land and take off in the dark, Buddy almost had to pinch himself make sure he was not dreaming but he did feel bad about the men they had to leave behind, including Dean, but when chosen to go you don't argue. It was a known fact. .They wanted to rescue pilots knowing that there outfits can do the most damage to the enemy that's what war is all about.

    They flew for about an hour when they felt the engines slow down and the plane touching down. They had landed, it taxiing for few minutes then stopped. The door opened again steps drop down. There were quite a few people to meet them on the ground vehicles escorting them to barracks where they had hot showers, hot food clean beds with lots of things to spoil you compared to what you had been through as a prisoner. The doctors were there to treat anybody who had been hurt or feeling ill. Some of the men were weak from malnutrition. Buddy was intense to see if Dean was amongst the other men that came in on a later flight, but he wasn't there. He didn't know what felt better the food or hot shower, but both were extremely welcomed. The next morning, right after breakfast they all went to interrogation where all the men, including Buddy, relayed their individual stories, experiences, how many guards etc. They wanted to know everything even the smallest detail.

Buddy gave all the information about his flight from one plane that got hit, the other one hopefully made it, he was sure that the bombs hit their target. He went on to let them know just about where he had been hit in Germany then you brought it that far, with one engine trying not to make a big thing about it of course, all of them could do their math, then went on to ask how they ended up at the prison camp where they were. If there had been contact with the underground in France. He relayed the fact about the farmer giving him the sign. Then he went on telling of his chance meeting with Wolf. They wanted detailed information he was trying to avoid the particular confrontation he had with that Nazi so-an-so. However they insisted he had to tell the story again. By this time everyone in the room, along with the men asking questions wanted to hear about this particular incident. Of course, when he was done with his account of what had happened. There was a similar reaction about the same as before. Also there were smiles on their faces, with lots of laughter. Buddy vowed he hoped he would never have to repeat this story again. With that done they were all informed that they would be returned to their outfits as soon as possible. This was good news to everyone, especially to Buddy because he still had unfinished business to accomplish now that he had more information than he ever had before.

CHAPTER SIX

The men along with Buddy that had been rescued were being transported to their bases they were talking about their experiences. They were glad to be back in England. Remembering the hospitality where they were wasn't so great. The conversation slowly died down, leaving each man to his own thoughts, Buddy kind of relaxed, starting to think about home. His family, he was wondering how things were with his mother, hoping she was okay. Wondering if she knew what had happened to him.

Paula woke up with a start she was having a dream. Naturally it was about Buddy being home. She could not go back to sleep so she decided to start doing things around her apartment, which she had for a while now, much to her brothers dismay. Paula felt she had to get her own place now that her brother was married, her name was Nonny. They had two kids, Roy and Nancy they love their aunt Paula who insisted that Jim and his family needed their privacy Nonny would just as soon had Paula live there with them. They enjoyed each other's company like they were sisters. It was good to have another woman to talk and share things with. It's hard to share certain things with a man even if he is your brother. Her apartment wasn't that far from where Jim lived with his family, of course he had to check on her often, maybe a little too often. Sometimes she felt he was taken his time away from his family. She was the only one that felt that way. Also he would bring the two children with him that would make her day. Deep inside, she wished she could have children, so she could spoil them like she does with her niece and nephew.

Paula started getting ready for work then thought about giving CT a call to see if he had heard anything from Buddy. Then she gave it a second thought maybe she called him too often to ask about her son that way. Every time she woke up quick like that she felt something was wrong. Her relationship with CT was as good as it was going to get, Paula knew with her past being what it was. She could not seem to move forward with their relationship. It's not that they had not tried, but every time she would freeze up and become ill. She also knew how frustrating this could be for Tom. He was such a gentleman she admired him for that with his tenderness towards her, telling her it was okay. He did know and understood about the issue about how Buddy came to be. There was such a thing as love without intimacy. She certainly knew what that was. This is the feeling she had for Tom. She could not wait to see him or be near him the way he held her. She felt very warm. Any time they were together, they would laugh and enjoy each other immensely. She felt giddy at times like a schoolgirl holding hands for the first time so they would just leave it at that. They both had become accustomed to that, but she always worried he was such a good-looking man. She often wondered why he settled for her. He could have any woman. She was sure he had offers from women that would put no restrictions on him like she did, Paula actually felt guilty at times about that. Then, on the other hand, she was terrified, because if she was in a position where she couldn't see him anymore or hear from him about things in Europe also about her son anyway, it was just terrifying even to think this way. Ever since Pearl Harbor there were a flood of young men signing up to serve. He was extremely overwhelmed with their training. He wanted nothing more than to get involved in the war himself. It was a constant battle within him. He knew how critical his training was for these young men having such a short time to train them to become pilots ready for combat now that we had enemies on both sides East and West. He didn't have much time off for socializing. He was really glad he had Paula she never demanded much from him. The time they had together was better than he had ever had with anyone else. He would never put pressure on her, or do anything to make her distrust him several times after they had eaten they would lie on the couch together, talking some times they would fall asleep in each other's arms, holding Paula close was very fulfilling for him she had warmth that he had never experienced. He thought to himself if he was married and had a family how would he be able to spend any quality time with them. Paula understood exactly what was expected of him and was glad even if their time together was sometimes limited. Life wasn't so bad after all. The best times were when they all were together for dinner especially during the holidays they would make a good meal and the children would always be glad to see Uncle Tom. They called him it was hard to explain to them at that age, but they accepted him anyway. As far as they were concerned that was Uncle Tom, since he had given her a ring. This was a promise rather than engagement ring. There were several reasons for this Paula had become manager of the store she was working in. That meant ordering large amount of products. She would have contact with salesmen that included having lunch with them sometime. Naturally, with her natural beauty, never wearing makeup, maybe just a light shade of lipstick, also wore fashionable, but not revealing clothing purposely to avoid attracting men in a provocative way she begin to realize as soon as men noticed she wasn't wearing a ring. They would ask her to go out on a date then there were the men that didn't care if you're wearing a ring. Realizing this, she bought herself a ring to wear on that finger hoping to stop men from advancing on her or asking her out. Tom had asked her about that so she explained the situation. One evening while they were alone, he presented her with a ring, saying I know that you refuse to get engaged or get married you say it's for my benefit. I understand, but this is a promise ring from me to you, a promise that I will always be there for you, Paula was beside herself. Tears welled up in her eyes as she promised him there will always be a warm place in my heart for you. One day while she was leaving a meeting she saw Tom with another woman. This woman was really pretty they were hugging, as they turned walking down the sidewalk arm in arm, laughing both involved with each other. Paula's heart sank. Knowing this was inevitable, Tom found himself another woman which she couldn't blame him. She tried to walk in the opposite direction, but Tom saw her. He hesitated for a moment then they walked up to her Tom introduced the woman. This is Laurie my sister from out of town. Laurie immediately grabbed Paula giving her a big hug, saying my sister Linda and I have heard so much about you through Tom's letters. It is great to finally meet you. Tom had said you were beautiful I'm almost jealous. They all laughed Paula was immediately relieved asking if she was moving here. She said no just visiting. With promises of seeing each other, spending time together, they left to go their separate ways

    Paula would hear of the devastation also the fighting in the air battles over Germany, France, England, what was it like for her son CT would try to calm her telling her the kind of training that Buddy had along with his extraordinary skills above most pilots. He would be able to out fly just about anybody he came up against out there. He certainly had the edge and that was valuable. Also, it is very hard to rattle somebody like him. Paula would always take comfort in what Tom would say about him.

    Then on the other side of this Jim and CT both had their heads together many times since CT had moved there with the training facilities right there at the airfield by the plant. They were able to compare their efforts, along with their notes, come up with innovations for new planes and older planes like Spitfires and Hurricanes and other British and American aircraft being used.

    Now they were feverishly working on modifying a new version of the fighter plane known as a P 51 Mustang, which had been on the drawing board for quite a while also some in production using them a lot for reconnaissance. They were an extremely good plane for low altitude flying between 14,000 and 15,000 feet. This plane being designed to fly long-distance it was fitted with auxiliary fuel tanks. This worked well for reconnaissance the problem was they didn't know how good it would do in battle it would fail at high altitudes, lacking the power. Along with this they were working on planes designed for aircraft carriers to fight against the Japanese zero, which was a formidable foe. By now the Americans had the edge. As far as training also their determination to fight, especially since Pearl Harbor, which was still fresh in everybody's mind. The Japanese had made a big mistake thinking that the Americans were a pushover and had no stomach for real combat. We were not considered warriors like some of the Japanese considered themselves as extreme fighters which proved to be their downfall.

    Jim and CT were both very excited about a new combined effort between the American and British aircraft they had come up with a idea to combine the P 51 fighter with installing a Rolls-Royce Merlin engine, there was some concern whether it could be done, however, they received and installed the Merlin engine putting them to the test, which proved to be excellent. They preformed beyond expectations with power acceleration, and altitude everything they had hoped for. This plane with its external fuel tanks was forming up to be the plane that could do bomber escort all the way into Germany and back. This would be a great milestone and protection because of the loss of planes without escort was becoming incredible high.

Both Jim and CT would really enjoy sharing this information, but they didn't dare to divulge a lot, you never knew when this could fall into enemy hands. No one wanted that kind of news to leak out the enemy would do everything in their power to stop anything of this magnitude to ever happen now more than ever, since they had not been able to bomb the British into submission. Buddy must have dozed off while he was reminiscing, he woke just in time to see they were entering his base area, excitement started rising just to know he was at his home away from home if you call it that, feeling kind of guilty in a way with a quick thought to everyone still in prison, wondering what kind of retribution they received after the escape. Right now he was definitely excited to be back, he said his goodbyes to the driver and the men he turned leaving the bus immediately got a big smile on his face, looking at a smiling face of his friend Whip, wondering how he knew to be there. It's very hard not to get close to someone, because you never know in this business from day-to-day, who's going to be there, but how could you not become friends with somebody like that and other men that you rely on every day. Whip grabbed Buddy by the arm and led him straight to the mess hall. He threw open the door then yelled hey guys look what I found, the Hawk is back. Everyone did their hoops and hollers and welcome back. It was chaotic for a few minutes, but it felt good to be welcomed back. Whip marched him right through the line, making sure he got plenty of food. They sat down at the table with the Maj. and Capt. Of course, it turned into a flurry of questions. How was it, what was it like, the major asking would you like to volunteer for another mission jokingly, Buddy smiled saying, I think I will wait for a day or so before I do that again. The Major said, I heard you had a visitor while you were there, Buddy stopped eating for a minute, looking at the Major shaking his head, knowing of his contact with intelligence then realizing no big surprise that he had heard about the encounter. Buddy asked what all did you hear, Maj. Morrison replied with a smile on his face. I thought they would have searched you several times for a gun. How did they miss that one referring to the fist with the finger and thumb, you probably wished it had been loaded about then, I think there would've been one less Nazi on this Earth. The whole place erupted in laughter. With that the Captain spoke up, we have a surprise for you tomorrow. In fact, there'll be a couple surprises tomorrow Buddy said you mean I have to wait till tomorrow the reply was, it will be worth the wait. With that Buddy said with a smile on his face it's very good to be back as he left, headed for his bunk, tomorrow will be a new day and a new beginning.

CHAPTER SEVEN

As he opened his eyes he was glad to see the American flag hanging where it was. This wasn't home, but you do get accustomed to the area you spend a lot of time in. The guys really wanted to give him some space, but they also wanted to know what it was like being captured. He was more than willing to talk about his experiences over what had happened. What it was like to be in a prison camp. He decided to give the guys a heads up about how the conditions were, how he felt bad having to leave them behind but he also realized telling them it was necessary. They consider pilots premium. Of course they wanted to hear about his meeting with Wolf, how that all went down, even though they'd heard it before they enjoyed hearing it again you think about it, how much joy do you get flying all the time. Seeing planes get shot down. All in all quite depressing so when you do give somebody a little something to raise their spirits you don't hesitate, just like Whip with his sense of humor.

The guys stayed late into the night making up for the time they were apart catching buddy up on all the latest , then the sad news. They had lost three more men it was inevitable but still hard to take. Buddy started to yawn. The men took that as a sign that he wanted to go sleep. He said no, not necessarily however it had been long day and that the yawn was involuntary. Whip said you just want to go to sleep so you can wake up early and see what the surprise is Buddy said to him, I guess you know all about it don't you, a couple the guys chimed in along with Whip saying yeah, we know what you're going to get. You deserve it whether you like it or not with that, they all left him to his thoughts. Whip whispered to Buddy you're really going to like this, he turned away laughing. As he laid down looking at the flag he thought to himself there should be two more flags up there one for the French resistance one for the moon squadron.

He was definitely up early the next morning doing everything he had to do even managed a few minutes for a good workout that he had missed while he was gone. It felt really good to warm up his muscles. He realized it would take him a little bit of time to work back to where he was before. He also noticed that there was more equipment, some new stuff that Axle had fixed up, one of the guys was a really good welder and was able to make up some very good weights. Maybe this was one of the surprises. After going through the line at mess hall he went to sit down at the table were he normally sat there was a package, he opened it quickly getting excited. There were two silver bars along with his notice of promotion. Whip yelled out if I get captured and spend some time in the prison camp maybe I'll get my promotion Buddy replied quickly, I'll gladly give you my second Lieut. Bars If you stay out of prison. Everyone laughed loudly. Maj. Morrison along with Capt. Harrison both congratulated him so did everyone else. Buddy thought to himself that was two very good surprises, his promotion also what they had done with his workout room. He was really happy as he left the mess hall headed toward the flight line. He was anxious to see Axle, the ground crew and Nigel who had helped him several times and was there most of time to help him strap in. As he walked out toward the planes he noticed that the Major and the Capt. were following him. They had a smile on their face. Also several other men were coming out, including Whip. As he approached where his Hurricane was normally parked, was a shiny Spitfire, Axle, Nigel and some of the ground crew were there offering their congratulations, Buddy with a big smile on his face shaking his head in disbelief, saying you are all guilty of spoiling me. Buddy noticed the decals below the canopy. There were a few Nazi signs meaning German airplanes, one decal stuck out more, it look like a mosquito dropping bombs then some Nazis with their eyeballs bugging out with their tongues hanging out, one of them even had a mustache, someone must've went to great lengths to make a decal like that. I don't know if I can handle all of this in one morning, I salute you all Axle said as he took what was left of his cigar out of the side of his mouth. Now are you going to be hard to deal with having your new silver bars Sir, with a smile also when you get done shining those bars I have an engine over here that needs timing, everyone roared with laughter, if you don't mind, "Sir" he said loudly while standing at attention with a snappy salute. Buddy smiled and replied gee, it's good to be back. I missed all this spit and polish stuff. As everyone was walking to the briefing room, Buddy remembered Axle was working on a Spitfire and needed someone to take it up to test so rather than call somebody from the barracks. He asked Buddy being he was right there if he would mind taking it up, of course he jumped at the chance. Once airborne he instantly felt the difference in power and the handling. It was a smaller plane, but responded quickly to his actions. He really felt at ease in this plane, probably had it up longer than he should have, when he brought it back down, bringing it back where Axle was he climbed out and stood there for a minute looking at the crew chief then smiled, shaking his head yes. So now that he had his own Spitfire, knowing that Axle had gone over it with a fine tooth comb doing the latest modifications it would run very good It could approach 400 mph or a little more, it should have no trouble keeping up with that FW. Briefing consisted of what it used to be, bomber escort. Buddy did want his revenge with Wolf. Now more than ever, but not at the cost of overpowering his duties to the men he was flying with also the mission they were assigned to do. There were new men assigned to this group. They were paired up with other fighters, but there always seemed to be one odd plane. So Buddy would lead two new guys which made them somewhat of a three some. So he had one on each side, just behind him. All three were Spitfires, so they were very closely matched up for speed and maneuverable tactics. He wasn't sure how much training they had or what each one was capable of, they were all nervous. He remembered all too well the first time for him also what they had said to him it seemed like yesterday, yet it also seemed like a long time ago, a lot had happened in that short period of time. He had told them before they left what it was like for him the first time, he hoped it would help. In the air flying across the channel, they hooked up with the bombers. Everything was a go as they maintained their speed, altitude, with one group a little higher. Someone yelled out specs in the distance heads up. Buddy, along with several other small groups accelerated to meet the specs head on the rest stayed back with the bombers. He told the other two men to stick with me as long as you can but make sure you cover each other, keeping his eyes toward the upper clouds, making sure they were not going to get jumped from a higher altitude also keeping a close watch out for that shiny plane being careful not to be drawn into a surprise attack. He saw two ME's heading for the bombers, Buddy with his two wing men took off after them. Between the three of them they made short work of the two ME's, and more fighters came in after the bombers. It was quite a skirmish for a while. By now they were well into French territory, one of the bombers had an engine smoking it was turning back toward England. Another bomber was going down in flames, but parachutes were coming out. Hopefully, they all got out as the planes slowly spiraled toward the ground and exploded. After the last encounter Buddy had accelerated climbing to a high altitude. The other two planes were below him. He saw two enemy planes one smoking that had broke off and headed away from the action. One of our planes flying with the bombers below them banked over took off after them. Sometimes this was not a good idea, Buddy felt this was one of those times, especially after he saw another one of our planes heading in that direction. So he immediately accelerated feeling the power of the Spitfire kicking in. He was in a real good dive accelerating trying to catch them. He was also calling over the radio trying to tell them to break it off and return to the bombers, but neither one of them did, gaining speed all the time looking around, waiting for an ambush to hit he started to feel the G forces then out of the corner of his eye he caught a glimpse of something like a blur coming fast, at the time he thought his mind playing tricks on him simply because whatever that was it's faster than anything he was accustomed to, when you're used to something fast like 350 or 400 miles an hour, and then something about 500 miles an hour comes by. You think you're seeing things but then you see puffs of smoke and fire in rapid succession coming out from the front end bullets tearing the fighter plane apart then hit a bomber destroying it in one sweep something like that isn't normal. Buddy remembered hearing that the Germans had been working on a jet propelled fighter that was supposed to be incredibly fast this had to be it. The plane was here in a flash then gone in a blur unbelievable, how do you compete with something like that, then it was back taking out the lead bomber, hoping the debris from it would take out other bombers that didn't happen this time. Those pilots were good. They didn't flinch. It was hard for bombers with all their guns to shoot at fighters at their normal speeds. There is no way they could hit this silver blur at that speed, you wouldn't even have enough time to aim let alone get a piece of it. Upon seeing this, Buddy automatically went into attack mode banking over hard going after the jet, knowing there was no way he could get anywhere near it, but he just wanted to get a shot at it. They had actually been briefed on this particular fighter. The new capabilities were awesome. But the downfall was the fuel consumption they could only stay in flight for a short period of time. Then it would have to land somewhere near for refueling. No one ever figured this plane would be in French territory. It should only be in Germany, where they could keep it in a shroud of secrecy also be protected, but it was here and now. There was a lot of chatter over the radio. Then someone popped up, sounded like Whip's voice. We have more company joining our party coming from the side. Guess who's leading them yep, it's that shiny plane looks like Wolf has come to join us. Buddy had pulled up to a higher altitude watching, wanting to see if there was a chance he could go after the jet, He really wanted Wolf, however he had other priorities right now dealing with this silver blur in the sky wondering how much fuel this guy had left, all these things are running through your head trying to figure out a plan Buddy noticed from his altitude that when that fighter swoop down, he would take out one of the bombers on the way down and then pull back up to hit another one in a short period of time. Buddy started calculating his mind working fast now; there might be a way to catch this jet at the bottom of his dive, then again at that speed that jet fighter would have quite a lot of drift with his speed, but he figured he could get to the bottom and catch him at the bottom. The jet fighter had to quit accelerating to slow down his descent before pulling back up. That's when it was at its slowest speed, so Buddy put his plane into a steep dive between the bombers just about the time the jet fighter was coming down. Hopefully, his timing was just right. He would only have a few seconds to accomplish this, he felt his Spitfire really come alive. He knew he was doing well over 400 mph, he cut back on the throttle just enough then he pulled back hard on the stick shoving the throttled back up again. The G forces were unreal like your body was being shoved through the bottom of the plane. About now that jet fighter had come down, taking out another bomber hitting the bottom of his loop just about the time Buddy's plane was pulling back up only a couple hundred yards away without even thinking. Buddy was pulling the trigger. He felt his plane shutter as the 20 mm cannons started going off. He watched the tracers incredibly near the jet fighter. He actually thought he saw for a split second couple rounds hitting the jet along with a small puff of smoke. Buddy never flinched, hoping against hope luck against luck the possibility that he had tagged a piece of the jet fighter of course this was only momentary because that fighter really poured the power on, he was out of there in a flash as Buddy pulled back up by the bombers losing sight of the jet, thinking to himself hopefully I'll get another shot at him. About that time somebody yelled out lookout Hawk there's somebody on your tail, it sounded like Whip again, I think you got a piece of the jet, someone else said, I saw a small stream of smoke or something coming from the side of it as it went past me, but I think you got problems that shiny plane is on you, along with another plane. Whip yelled out hang on, I'm coming down about that time, Buddy felt something hit the side of his plane automatically went into some evasive maneuvers skidding sideways coming over backwards his reactions were faster than his mind. He knew he had an advantage with the Spitfire being quite a bit faster, knowing also Wolf's plane was fast. Also no telling who was with him in the other plane with no time or elevation to do that loop again. All he could do was outmaneuver these two about that time he saw someone coming straight at them. He was hoping it was one of our planes, Buddy headed straight at the oncoming plane. There were only a few hundred yards away from each other now. It was still coming as it went past him. The plane started firing past him. He caught a quick glimpse at who was flying that one sure enough it was Whip Buddy got a smile on his face, shaking his head. That guy sure has guts. I'm glad he's on our side. He couldn't see behind him, but he was sure the enemy plane got the worst of it as he rolled over top backward. He got a quick look upside down. He could see the enemy plane in a ball of fire heading for the ground he lost sight of Whip. Then a few more tracers went by the side of his plane, he kicked it hard skidding sideways, not letting anybody get a clear shot at him, so he banked into a hard left hand turn. He might get lucky enough with the speed to get in behind Wolf and again he was doing all this ahead of his thoughts. It was a little bit of help, knowing the other plane wasn't after him. As Buddy was doing these maneuvers a thought crossed his mind. Why two of them were after him and not the bombers. You would've thought Wolf himself would be enough to go after someone. Something just didn't add up about all this. Maybe it was because he went after the jet fighter I'm sure this was a priority again, why was this highly secret plane in French territory? Buddy put his Spitfire in a steep dive then started making inside loops, then banked hard to the left coming around increased his speed, G forces, throwing him against the bottom of the plane again, wondered if Wolf was having the same reaction, although what he saw of him at the prison camp in the dim light. He was in decent shape Buddy had noticed they were similar in height, weight, looking fairly similar in build, except Buddy was a bit taller. He remembered Wolf stretching himself a little bit taller, trying to look eyeball to eyeball it seemed to unnerve him a little bit not being used to looking up at someone, but he got a slight smile on his face, remembering. As Buddy started in a hard circle to the left he almost felt like he was gaining on that FW, not a lot, but significantly. He definitely kept up the chase after several minutes of this Buddy had gained almost half the distance. It was clear by now that in time, he would be the one doing the firing at that shiny plane it would be a shame to get that plane all dirty with bullet holes. Suddenly the plane he was chasing leveled off, made a hard right then a role trying to come back around to reverse a situation, Buddy wasn't letting that happen he was ready for him. He actually threw a couple more rounds at the German plane just to shake him up but it was an immediate opposite roll, then bank to the right, hoping to evade more rounds. Buddy then held steady, waiting to see what his next move was keeping his throttle up inching closer kicking the plane to the left a little trying to strafe across the German plane he was back far enough not to know for sure, he thought maybe, just one or two rounds made contact with him. Buddy decided not to use any more ammo until he got closer, it was hard to keep track. He did not run out, continued following making counter maneuvers against what

Wolf was doing every once in a while he would throw a few rounds over there just to rattle him a little. Then would come some more radical moves a little different than what Wolf usually did. For a while, Buddy was almost convinced that there was something wrong with the plane he was following. Wondering if he was having some mechanical problems, lookout he thought to himself. The ground crew had screwed up on his plane, there would be trouble. Heads will roll if that was the case. The other thing was this is the first time he's been up against Wolf. since he started flying the Spitfire, so he decided it was time to go on a full-scale attack he made every move count, being very aggressive also a lot closer now. He wasted no time blasting away at every move the enemy plane made he was right there waiting for him. He started firing more often, but still on guard, knowing that Wolf would double back on you. He was ready for him. In fact, that's the kind move he was expecting but when it didn't happen, he wasn't sure what to expect, but then he didn't care. He was poised; ready to do damage. This was pilot against pilot machine against machine would this be the day of the Scarf he reached up and grabbed it quickly, then reach back down for the throttle his finger ready. A moment later, he had his chance. The FW leveled off for just a second. Buddy shot off some rounds to the left side, automatically kicking the plane to the right his bullets and tracers were finding their mark as the plane in front of him rolled right into his line of fire. The FW started smoking, continuing to roll over upside down, Buddy fired some more into the upside down plane, smoke and flames pouring out now as it headed towards the ground. He was waiting for the canopy to come back or fly off and the parachute to come out, as the plane nosedived faster now heading straight down. A lot of chatter was coming over the radio. Somebody was saying, the Hawk got the Wolf, the Yanks got the Wolf, it's going down he followed the plane down it spiraled a few times then crashed head-on into the earth in a big ball of flames. There was a lot of different yelling over the radio yeah, yeah over the radio, the Wolf is dead the Wolf is dead. The dirty dog has bit the dust. Did anyone see a parachute another voice said no, no parachute that's good I might have had to go after it I'm glad I don't have to now Buddy circled the ground a few times making sure, but there was no way anyone walking away from that, after a few minutes he saw some figures coming out of the bushes toward the smoldering wreckage, they could tell it was a German plane, what was left of it, as they looked up and saw the Spitfire a couple of them took potshots at him. Buddy pulled back on the stick throttled up to get away. That's all I need, some guy with a rifle getting lucky shot bringing him down. By now, the bombers had moved on, the call came over the radio for everyone to break off, that's what everybody did at the moment there was no air combat taking place. The remaining FWs and MEs had moved on, the battle was over for now. Excitement levels were pretty high. Buddy felt good about what had transpired. He couldn't help thinking again replaying everything that happened, why the plane he was chasing banked right into his line of fire. He really wanted to celebrate along with the rest of the guys. The chatter over the radio was total excitement, several planes surrounded him. Of course, one was his buddy Whip with a big smile shooting something with his hand, then making a circle, pointing down Buddy had to laugh, shaking his head as he looked to the other side. Another pilot was given him a thumbs-up. Nobody could blame them It was hard enough to deal with the enemy that you come up against that were good pilots, but nobody wanted to be a victim of Wolf's vicious attack. As they progressed back toward the base he had time to think. Wondering who the high ranking officer they had chose to fly that jet then the thought came into his head Lord help us if Wolf ever gets his hands on something like that, but we won't have to worry about that no more. His thoughts drifted to his mother hoping there was a possibility that his death would have released her from the grip this had on her and created a miracle now allowing her to have a normal life, maybe even with CT that would be the greatest thing about all this, but there was still something nagging at him about all that had happened, something still did not add up what if Wolf had been flying that jet, then who was flying his plane, he wouldn't let just anyone take his precious shiny machine. Another thought occurred to him the way that fighter had taken out those bombers along with a couple fighters. That was a pattern you'd expect from somebody like Wolf. The only thing different was the pilot following them down didn't drill more holes, trying to kill the rest of the crew. But then with that type of machine, you only have so much fuel with so much time in the air. Would someone like him be able to control himself. After landing along with many congratulations from other pilots and ground crew, Axle standing away from the planes lit a cigar, saying this was a good time to celebrate. We have a lot to talk about later. Smiling Buddy pointed at his Spitfire with a thumbs-up, shaking his head yes as he headed straight for debriefing, knowing ahead of time what that was going to be like. Naturally it was all about the jet fighter as many details about it as possible. This was crucial information Buddy again trying to downplay all the attention, saying he just got lucky maybe it was one of the gunners in the bomber group. They were all shooting at the fighter maybe one of them got a shot at it. He sure wanted those guys to get some credit in the middle of all this. After all, they were sitting ducks. Everyone knew better, but they wanted to know in detail how he was able to achieve what he had done, but it was very important for times in the future if someone had the chance to do exactly that same maneuver. Of course losing three of their own men and planes also bomber crews put a damper on some of the celebration. Maybe, just maybe, some of them were able to parachute out. We could only hope, a couple men said yes they did see some parachutes. But the one they were glad not to see was the one that didn't come out of the shiny plane. There was a loud roar of agreement to that. Debriefing over the natural thing to do was head for the mess hall. Everyone was extremely hungry. Celebrating always made a person hungry everyone except Buddy. As he sat down across from Capt. Harrison and a few of his fellow pilots he had kind of a light smile on his face. Someone mentioned you don't seem to be very excited about what had happened. I would think you would be more excited than the rest of us, Buddy replied. I really wish I could he said. I just wish I could. Capt. Harrison said something is on your mind. Yes he replied. Only time will tell I just hope nobody will be disappointed, the last thing I want is to let anybody down Wolf landed the jet cautiously. It was a whole lot harder to land, then the conventional propeller planes. You have to maintain more speed and it needed a lot more length to bring it in. But the benefit of this plane outweighs everything. Wolf was beside himself with excitement. He was amazed how many planes he was able to knock down in a single run if they could just control the fuel consumption or just be able to carry more that would be incredible. This will turn the tide and we will be able to conquer anyone we please, that means anyone. This was actually his first combat flight in this area. He had been able to take one up before, after some intense training just to learn how to take off, also control and land this magnificent machine Wolf had pleaded for months to take this into France to be able to stop the bombers from reaching Germany. With 10 of these machines he could surely do that. He could prove this if they would just let him but all his pleading fell on deaf ears. They did not want this plane out of their territory no way no how, if something should happen and one these would fall in the hands of the allies against Germany it would be disastrous. As it was Germany was way behind in this war now that the Americans had got totally involved, which only made Wolf's argument more important, he would demand twice as much security and many more conventional planes to help guard these, but in the long run his arguments failed, this order came down from the highest command the man himself. The Fuhrer Wolf had decided the only thing to do was just to take it. And that's exactly what he did. No one was telling him what he could do. Thinking when he proved his point then he would be a hero. It took some time to set this up because he had planned to somehow fly it there. So he did this, it took awhile but he accomplished it. Of course, bringing the fuel was another challenge that he overcame also. The high command was up to their necks trying to figure out how to stop everything from closing in on them. Some of them even knew the end was not so far away several assassinations attempts had failed. He had found an area that had a long stretch of straight road in France. There was also a bunker that the French had used to store very large equipment. It was perfect. Wolf was extremely proud of himself. It was like he was running his own country, and war to satisfy himself. He had assembled a large amount of soldiers, also maintenance crew. He had become a full colonel with that he gained a certain amount of power. As he inspected his plane, he realized someone had hit him with a lucky shot. There was a small amount of oil down the side of the fuselage where the smoke had come from. He was extremely upset about this. He certainly did not want any one out of his realm to know about this. Wolf also knew who was responsible for this it had to be to that American. If He knew that this person was going to be able to escape, he would've shot him then and there, no matter what the consequences would've been now you had to deal with this. Wolf went to debriefing all he did was brag about how many planes he'd shot down, emphasizing on the bombers probably more than he actually did. He was taking credit for some of the bombers the other planes had shot down this information took quite a while. Once the proceedings were over, he headed to the barracks, this is when he found out his plane had been shot down and the pilot had been killed. Wolf was stunned, realizing the gravity of the situation now. It was also confirmed that it was the HAWK that had shot down his FW.

Remembering the conversation he had that morning with his friend Hans that his plane was not in operation, so he couldn't go up. Wolf really wanted Hans with him that day to show him how good the jet fighter preformed also using him as a witness to how valuable this plane would be to back up his reasoning for taking it that far from Germany and he needed his friend, more than ever. He asked them over and over. If it was true, realizing it had to be because Hans had not made it back. Wolf was so excited about his accomplishments. He had failed to even recognize the fact that his one and only friend wasn't with him at debriefing. It was told over and over to him the same story. It was the Yank that had done it also there was no parachute that it had crashed into the ground exploding every time someone said that it was like he was being slapped in the face. Wolf stormed to his barracks screaming in German. I should have killed him. I should have killed him; again, and again with his stupid little finger, acting like he had a gun. If I had him here now I would choke him, punish him for what he had done. For once in his life he felt very alone and rather small. He grabbed his bottle of cognac and started drinking. He finished the bottle slamming it against the door, grabbed another bottle started drinking it as he sat down on his bed. He had never done this before, never lost control like this. He slid in and out of consciousness. He had only one thought that was to kill the Yank with that Scarlet Scarf was he trying to mock me. I will strangle him with it was his last thought before he passed out.

CHAPTER EIGHT

Celebrations went long into the evening. The men needed something to let their hair down what had happened today was just the right time. It had started raining very heavy overcast meaning only one thing, there would be no flying. The next day the whole countryside would be socked in, so it was a good excuse as any, after some time celebrating, Buddy excused himself heading to his bunk area he just could not get into the mood to celebrate as he sat on his bunk. He took off the scarf looking at it with disdain. He threw it on the bed beside him. About then Whip sat down across from him saying "trouble in paradise", you should be more elated after what had happened today. And what's with the scarf are you mad at it also isn't that your favorite scarf you wear it all the time, Buddy did give a slight smile on his face replying. I will tell you about it sometime, but right now if I felt like celebrating. Trust me, the scarf would be gone. I'm very upset right now about what I saw today that fighter came out of nowhere, slammed a bunch of fighters, bombers, and then was gone. Yeah, I had a chance shot at it, but there's no way you can defend against that. Whip totally agreed with Buddy saying I sure don't want to go up against one, but if I had to I wouldn't hesitate. Buddy said I have no doubt in my mind that you would. You've been flying longer also have seen a lot more than I have. I look up to you for that. You came through for me today taking that Nazi off my back I was worried for a minute that you were after me. But then that wouldn't look to good up there on your fuselage with all those Nazi signs and then to have a British sign to. Whip replied I feel the same about you I 'm just glad you're on our side now that we got that all done and said let's go have a pint of ale to celebrate, looking at each other then they both laughed. Buddy said to Whip, if he is the one that was in the plane. Then he and scarf will both be gone then we can celebrate like we have never done before. In fact, they'll have to order more ale for us, but for now, why not let's go have a pint Just because.

As Buddy approached planes the next morning, knowing they weren't going to fly with the overcast he wanted to talk to Axle, approaching the area he saw the ground crew working on a lot of different planes. Now with downtime is a good time to do a lot of maintenance. Also, this was good for him to work on his Spitfire as a voice behind him, which was Axle, saying with his hand extended congratulations on yesterday, there's always pride knowing when one of their planes took down the Wolf also a possibility of catching a piece of the jet, Axle went on to say, I can't even imagine what it would be like to go up against something like that. Buddy replied back. It's amazing the speed of that fighter is unbelievable. I imagine it's a little hard to control, at that speed, it has a limited fuel range, but it sure as hell, took out quite a few of our planes in the short period of time it was up, Axle had a bit of a smile on his face he had never heard Buddy swear if you could call that swearing, but he could understand the frustration of any pilot, not being able to go up against something like that. By the way, he said to Axle did you do something to that Spitfire, it seems like it was little faster than the one I took up before. The crew chief kind of chuckled, declaring the fact that they did some modifications on that particular engine. So you noticed, I take it Buddy replied yes, so what am I your guinea pig now, if I am when you have anymore of those little tricks feel free to use them on my plane. They both laughed, wave me down if you need anything with a loud Sir smiling as he walked away. Buddy was getting into the engine compartment, checking things out when he happened to look up to see Whip heading his way Buddy buckled up the engine cover then jumped down off the wing walking toward him. The Major wants to see you Whip said quietly they headed to the buildings. The walk was fairly quiet. Buddy had somewhat of an idea of what was coming, thinking to himself this is about Wolf. Buddy tried to make small talk a couple times on the way back Whip's answers were, right to the point with not a lot of humor unlike him, as they entered the building It was fairly quiet compared to when he left, the excitement level wasn't there. Buddy sat down across from Maj. Morrison, along with several other men, including the Captain.

Everyone seemed to have a solemn face as they broke the news to him that the plane he had shot down had definitely been Wolf's plane, however he wasn't flying that one. It was his best friend Hans, who was a well seasoned pilot himself, who has been flying longer than Wolf, he actually taught Wolf how to fly, but somehow he outranked Hans. No one knew how he ended up in Wolf's plane, but intelligence was pretty firm about the fact that Wolf was actually flying the jet fighter. Buddy spoke up saying I was afraid of that. The Capt. said, you knew something didn't you. Yes, he replied, somehow I knew that wasn't Wolf I had shot down but I didn't know for sure if that was him or some high ranking officer flying the jet. My other question would be why is that plane so far away from Germany there's no way he could have taken off from their country flew that distance in France then fly back, I know for a fact that they don't have that range.

The major spoke. We are sure he has it stashed in France someplace, you can bet under heavy guard through intelligence we know this is the only jet plane outside of Germany. The reports are a bit sketchy right now. We are hoping to have more answers later. Right now you have a big problem on your hands Wolf will be crazy mad like a rabid dog because of what you have done to his friend also you got a piece of that jet according to the reports of the few men that were there confirming a bit of smoke coming off that plane. So he's going to be really outraged about both incidents you would be his number one target, that jet fighter with its speed, you will be in trouble up there. Of course their main objective is to knock out the bombers. That's their priority, but with him. He has his own priorities, you know that.

Maj. Morrison went on to inform Buddy what we're doing is trying to compile information about this fighter naturally It's our priority. They have been seen in Germany a few times, so were trying to question our pilots that have been close to or went after one of these, you are one of them. We want your input. Buddy got very emotional. His eyes turn steel gray, his hands tight on the table, leaned forward, saying there's no way in hell that we can do anything to defend against something like this. It had to be at least 100 miles an hour faster than anything we have up there. Everyone else saw what I saw. I did what I thought was the best and only way I knew how to get a shot at it. Catch it at its weakest spot evidentially I was lucky enough to do that. Buddy continued, if I was flying that plane. I would definitely go after the bombers knock down as many as possible, I would go high come down as fast as I could with the advantage of speed, even though they're already fast it would be hard for anyone to get a shot at you. So you have to cut your speed right at the bombers on your downward loop to be able to come back up and stay in the area, because with that speed along with your drift you could be a long ways away from your objective real fast. The damage he accomplished with one plane in a short period of time. You can only imagine with his caliber of flying also men like him what they would do with a gaggle of these they could easily wipe out a squadron of our planes. Buddy finished with. I hate to repeat myself, but how the hell can you defend yourself or anybody else against something like that other pilots voiced their opinions very much similar to what he was saying. As he stood up, he said. I apologize if I have been out of line, speaking like this, but this is how I feel. With that, he left the building.

Buddy headed straight for the workout room knowing he had to work off some frustration also loosen up his body. After some time of working out he looked up as the door opened, a hat come flying in the room. Buddy wondered what that was all about, then a face appeared around the door of course it had to be Whip with a smile on his face I wanted to see if my hat, survived the attack before I came in, Buddy smiled and then started to laugh. He really needed this about now, his friend always seem to know how to take the tension off.

Whip said just one more thing of caution now for sure what it's going to be like up there, Wolf will be after you. I'll be up there right along with everybody else. I'll do my best to help anyway I can. Buddy replied. I know you will. I can count on that. Together we make a good team, then with a smile on his face, but you still make me nervous when you come straight at me with your guns wide open, his friend replied back just please, promise me one thing, when I do that. Don't ever sneeze. I think maybe we will both bite the dust if that happens, they both laughed as other pilots came in to join them saying, let us in we'd like to have a good laugh to, they also realized how important it was to work out. Keeping your body in shape helps you, especially if you have two maybe three missions a day, which did happen, you would crawl out of your plane down off the wing and collapse right there, even your mind would be tired, asking the ground crew when they came to service your plane bring me a pint of ale and my bed in that order Please. After the workout, talking with the other pilots relaxing, getting that calm nature back also a good shower Buddy laid down on his bunk, letting things go through his mind, after getting things off his chest, realizing he still had a job to do, along with his ulterior motive, which was to bring some serious pain actually eliminate Wolf in retaliation for the pain he had caused his mother along with other people no doubt. Also, now more than ever becoming more personally involved with this countries struggle to survive coping with the everyday effort just to stay alive.

Buddy heard a voice coming out of the radio watch out the Wolf is on your tail, he automatically started doing his evasive maneuvers. He was throwing everything he could, at that Spitfire he could to out run the Wolf. Who was also doing his maneuvers to keep up with the Spitfire he seemed to be right on Buddy's tail making some rounds hit the back of his plane, Buddy decided to do a steep dive with several spirals, then pulled hard on the stick back up out of it, but Wolf seemed to anticipated every move, someone it sounded like Whip came over the radio again, announcing the Wolf is getting closer, as the Spitfire received more rounds. Buddy's worst fears were coming true as he went into another dive. Some of the rounds had come through the canopy hitting his arm with severe pain. Another couple rounds hit the engine, smoke was coming out. Buddy threw open the canopy to clear some of the smoke. A huge rush of air pounding him Wolf was right there on every turn with an evil grin, victory was very near, savoring every moment, every round that went into the Yanks plane in front of him noticing the canopy had come open. He anticipated the pilot to bail out, he was ready for that to happen then he would have a clear shot directly at him with no mercy. He would gladly blow this person apart. He should never have killed his friend Hans. Buddy's plane was rushing toward the ground at a high rate of speed. He thought to himself he had to get out of there somehow. So he tried to bail out, but for some reason he was stuck in the plane hooked on something unable to get out his fate sealed, as his plane hurtled toward the Earth with certain death with a quick thought how long does it take you to die. How was his mother going to take this would she know who had done this to him. He hoped she wouldn't find out. That would really devastate her along with his uncle Jim and CT, it wouldn't be good. He braced himself for the impact as the trees loomed in front of him. As Buddy reached up to grab the Scarlet Scarf he knew it was over. Then with a deep breath he woke up. Of course he had been in a deep sleep, he sat up in bed, swung his feet over the side of the bed, his head in his hands. He was in a cold sweat, heart pounding, it sure felt real, taking a few minutes to come out of it, his heart still racing. One of the men said bad dream right, Buddy said yes continuing they seem so real and then you wake up, the other guy said I guess I'm not the only one and yes, they sure feel real when it's happening you wake up to check yourself. See if you're still alive and breathing or slammed into the ground in a pile of rubble, smoke fire, dust, or you messed your pants. After showering he came back to his bunk area, he had calmed down some but it's still fresh in your mind, as you realize there's always a possibility it could really happen. After receiving news of some stand down time, Buddy headed to the flight line to work on his plane, he enjoyed that almost as much as he enjoyed flying. He certainly wanted his plane to fly and handle as good as possible, knowing if he had to go up against Wolf or the jet again, although no match, his plane would still be in top flying condition against the other planes. While working on this Spitfire Axle joined him, wanting to talk about the jet fighter, the weaknesses as Buddy explained to the crew chief when you're up there, you realize what you're up against you really have to study the situation. Even though you don't have time, you still have to also wishing someone would know where they were trying to set up production for these then have someone drop a big egg right on top of their plant. After he and Axle finished working on a project they came up quite successful, the crew chief announced. If you were not such a good pilot I think we would have you transferred to maintenance I think we would be a good team, Buddy replied if I had failed flight school, that's probably where I would've ended up. Working on these planes is my second favorite thing to do. As anyone can tell only by the grease on your hands and the end of your nose they both laughed. About a week when they got called to go up for bomber escort which ended up being fairly routine It seems like Germany had exhausted some of their best pilots on this great effort they had in this Battle against Britain. It almost seemed like the pilots they were sending up with their FWS and ME's were younger, less experienced flyers. You could tell, most of our men were racking up some good scores against the enemy. Also we were not losing as many of our planes as before that was really good news. This included Buddy, all the while wondering why they hadn't been slammed by that jet fighter anymore or Wolf, everybody wondered what had happened, but also elated because of it. This seemed to continue for quite some time. They were almost in a relaxed state, but still always on alert. Buddy, along with other senior pilot's were wing men for younger pilots so they could get some experience, but always there to back them up. This was given us a great edge. Finally, the news came down through intelligence channels. They had found out that Wolf had more or less taken that jet into France without permission. The high command finally realized what had happened and censored Wolf back to the interior of Germany. In fact, it was so bad he was ordered to fly in one of his FWS restricting him from using the jet fighter, but from what we understand the alternative was to be shot by Hitler, who went into a rage, nearly berserk when he found out one of his precious jet fighters was in a foreign country also had sustained some bullet holes. He wanted to kill Wolf himself except he was smart enough to remember what an exceptional pilot he was also they had to admit when he did have that particular plane in France He did inflict a lot of damage to the bombers and fighters in his path. Because of that Wolf was still alive. That also brought the question up what if they had a bunch of those fighters in France, would the extent of damage to the bombers outweigh the possibility that one of these could fall into the wrong hands. On the other side of things France was still under German control. Except for the French underground that was still actively working in this area. Of course if they got their hands on one of these, they would do everything to use it against the Germans: two win their country back. Bomber escort was working quite well on this side of Germany. However once they crossed that line into Germany things changed dramatically our fighters had to turn back, our fuel wouldn't carry them any further, so they were at the mercy of the FWS and MES also the jet fighters. They were racking up an enormous amount of our planes being shot down, losing a lot of men, of course, mainly due to the new plane in the German arsenal that was almost impossible to shoot at from a bomber. Not that they weren't good shots, how can you shoot something you can't see. It seemed like every day there were more and more of them this went on for months the only relief was when they had to stand down because of weather. There had to be some way to stop them. The answer came a while later. Maj. Morrison announced after the days debriefing if anyone wanted to do some night flying. There was something urgent that needed to be taking care of. Let me know later if any of you want to volunteer. A couple of guys looked at Buddy of course he did just that, along with a couple other men. Asking the major what do you have in mind? The Major replied some reconnaissance, you have to fly at night then take the pictures in the first daylight hours. That's all I can tell you about it. The rest would be covered when you get there. After all was said and done, Buddy seemed to be the only one interested then was told he would repeat what he had done the last time also to report to Capt. Mudd again, just like before, so he packed his bags again, caught the transportation the next morning wondering what this mission was going to be like. Buddy could only wish it had something to do with the major problem that was facing them also, maybe a chance to fly that wooden wonder again. He really enjoyed that plane even as much as flying his Spitfire. It would be great if it had something to do with that jet fighter, no matter what he was committed no doubt about that.

CHAPTER NINE

The next day after being transported, Buddy reported to Capt. Mudd as ordered. After the customary salute the Capt told Buddy to relax, have a seat. I was hoping maybe they would send you or that you would volunteer. We really need somebody to do a specialized job, along with one other plane, Buddy replied, does the order have anything to do with that Wooden wonder, the Capt. got a smile on his face then replied yes, we like these planes for this particular job, Buddy replied, count me in, the Capt. said you haven't heard what you have to do yet, Buddy replied again. It doesn't matter, I'm in. There was a knock at the door. Another pilot entered the room, reporting, I'm Lieut. Teal, Then the Capt. Introduced the two of them. Now, that I have both of you here. Your mission will be to go to a certain area to do some reconnaissance. I can't tell you how serious this is. There's an ordinance plant we think they are producing jet fuel, we're not sure how far along they are, but it's critical. That's why we need two planes with different angles to be sure you will fly at night just before dawn. Your timing would be important with early morning light just after dawn should give us what we need the other problem, this plant is between two mountains. That's why they picked this particular place you will be flying at each other with not much room for error. So this is what you're up against. I have to know now if you both accept this mission both pilots agreed at the same time, Buddy had a smile saying I've been up against these jet fighters, it seems like we have to do some thing, well here it is. You can count me in, Lieut. Teal spoke up I'm in also the Capt. said good consider the rest taking care of.

The next evening they entered the hanger, three Mosquitos were setting there also Dean was standing there Buddy was real surprised and very glad to see him. They shook hands, had several minutes of conversation to catch up on how he got out of prison also if he was on this mission, Dean replied. I'm on backup in case something goes wrong then I have to repeat what you two are doing. The Capt. said, we have final details to go over, Buddy you are going around, coming from the north. This will be a surprise for them Lieut. Teal will be coming from the other direction, trying to coordinate both flights meeting at the same place the same time totally confusing them, then get out of there as fast as possible then back here. This is clear to both of you? They both replied yes. Well then good hunting. Buddy, Dean and Teal went to their designated area. They had some time before nightfall as they eat Dean commenced to tell that the prisoner still laugh about what you did. They talk about it every day it seems to bring their spirits up even though it was old news by now, Buddy was glad.

    The flight went as planned everything seemed to be right on the money. There was a bit of flak, but it was at a higher altitude. We came in low to get good pictures. So we were in there real fast both pilots were flying right at each other. They were right there was no room for error. Then the long flight back. Flying low and easy on the way there, so on the way back we opened them up, fast and hard to get back if anyone came up. It would be pretty hard for them to catch us however, Buddy wondered what it would be like to fly one in a combat mission. He thought to himself. It would be interesting, but under no circumstances were they to get involve in any confrontation with this mission. Once we landed then taxied over to the hangers coming to a stop they were already pulling the cameras out. Buddy and Teal both examined their planes noticing there were a few small minor holes. Whatever they did, evidently it was right.

Both pilots after checking their planes headed back to the barracks for a long rest after the long night of flying. That afternoon, Buddy decided to do some running as he always like to do, when he came back to the barracks area Capt. Mudd was talking with Lieut. Teal, so he included Buddy in the conversation thanking both of them for an excellent job the pictures were very informative. In fact it proved that the Germans were further ahead than what they thought, that they were already producing fuel for the fighters. So this is a matter of great importance. We plan to go back and bomb this facility as soon as possible, hopefully within 48 hours. That's if we get it all together in time. There's no doubt it has to be done as Buddy listened intently thinking in the back of his mind asking the Capt. are you going to use the same type of planes again, why are you interested said Capt. Mudd, Buddy's reply was I might be, Lieut. Teal spoke up. I just might be also, both pilots agreed. This has to be done. We've been there we're familiar with the flight let us do this, Buddy was in total agreement. The Capt.'s reply was, I'll get back to you later today. As far as I'm concerned it's a done deal. This time however you're going to be hit with a lot more flak and maybe some fighters with night radar, being you've been there, they're going to be ready for us. I'll talk to both you later. The next evening they assembled in the hangers as they had done before getting all the information being introduced. Buddy's, navigator was Craig, who had been on quite a few missions, knowing they picked someone with good experience also high qualifications for this type of mission because they were the lead plane. Teal's navigator was a guy called Blaine. Who had worked closely with Craig on some critical jobs in the past, so they spent some time together, getting acquainted. Always good to talk amongst each other what was expected of them along with their flight plan also what to do just in case something should go wrong.

The flight went as expected, it was a long flight, just as the flight before, lots of time to think to himself, wondering how many other facilities they had producing this type of fuel, with luck they would be able to knock them out, the Germans were smart enough not to have everything in one place. One thing good about this flight it was all done at night. That meant right now there were no fighters out there to worry about on our way there, then the light came on meaning Craig was taking over. He was guiding the plane to drop the bombs. Both planes carried two 500 pound bombs, Buddy figured that we were right on target all the way. When Craig took over, there wasn't much variation in our flight then all hell broke loose. The night was lit up with explosions, flak had started, the plane was bouncing around Greg held the plane on course, then the light came on indicating he was ready to drop the bombs. Buddy knew when they were dropped. He felt the plane lift as a thousand pounds of weight was lifted off. It felt good to let them go Buddy shoved the throttle hard as he banked hard to the right they saw the bombs explode. Then there were two more explosions then a big ball of fire followed.Now is time to get out of there as they climbed through the flak the plane shook really hard a couple times, he was sure that they had picked up some shrapnel from them. However, everything seemed to be working okay, he did notice one of the flaps was a little sticky, Buddy was still able to maneuver also pull up, they were climbing, trying to go over 30,000 feet, another blast of explosions Buddy hoped the plane in back of them was still there he decide to take a chance they were being shot at anyway. So he called out to the other plane. Yes, he came back on the radio, we took a hit in the Buddy replied we took some to but we're okay, let's get out of here I'm right behind you. I think we did okay back there "you bet" came back the reply I don't think they're real happy with us right now. Everything seemed to settle down for a while as they headed back toward England. Hoping to reach their before daylight. They didn't need to get into a fight right now. Craig came over the radio saying he was sure we nailed that back there, now all we have to do is get back. We don't have a lot of armament to get into a battle with a shiny plane or a jet. After some time of flying coming close to the French border the sky lit up in front of and all around them then, heavy flak with powerful spotlights, almost like they were waiting for some planes to come through this area, Buddy instantly tried to climb up they seam to follow him with more explosions. Then he felt something hit the side just behind him. He also felt something hit his leg then right near the engine as the plane shuddered hard. It was getting difficult to maintain a straight line then they sustained a few more hits the right engine started smoking. He could see it with the spotlights and more explosions from flak then fire started coming out, thinking here we go again. So he feathered the engine then shut it down. Buddy did this all automatic. After about 10 min. of this, things seem to quiet down for the moment he was trying to assess his situation, which wasn't very good trying to reach Craig behind him, but no answer. Now traveling with one engine slowed everything down. He wasn't quite sure exactly where they were there was no way to tell. He just flew the plane in the general direction of which they had been heading according to his compass. Hoping it was right now I wasn't sure of anything, except they were still in the air again, wondering if Teal was still behind him. I was the lead plane so they were trying to pick me off then go after the other plane. Time was against them now if the flack wasn't enough, the slower they went the closer to daylight that was their biggest enemy right now. Maybe there were planes already in the air. Look for them. Several of the German planes now had decent night vision radar but it had limitations for distance, however, the enemy knew where they came from also where they were headed that was no mystery. Buddy concentrated on the immediate problems right now. Also, there was an eerie quietness behind him where Craig was, he felt something warm going down his leg the pain was worse. About that time he saw some thing beside him it shook him for a second. Then he realized it was the other plane was flashing signals at him having nothing to signal back with, both hands were busy. He took a chance by turning on the radio hopefully he still had it on short-range asking are we on, yes the reply came back we see you have one engine, also had slowed down considerably. Are you hanging in there? Buddy replied so far so good. I can't reach Craig. It's a quiet back there. The voice came back over the radio. You have some damage right where he was sitting your engine must've been hit at the same time. Buddy called back to the other plane are we headed in the right direction. Also how far away from the channel, the voice came back. Yes, were headed in the right direction. We are also an hour or so from the coastline. Do you think you can make it? I doubt it, but I'm going to try to get as close as I can. You know, it will be daylight soon, as slow as were going it's going to happen before we get to the coastline then there will be plenty of enemy planes after us, you should go on. We decided to stay with you for a while we're okay at the moment we still have speed if we needed to get out. You are starting to lose altitude. Yes, Buddy replied. I'm glad we had climbed to get away from flak right now at the rate I'm losing it won't be too long before I might have put it down. It would be nice to see some smiling British faces or French ones, when I do but I don't think that's going to happen. I'll probably be looking at some nasty looking German faces like before. As they flew in silence for some time his plane still shaking hard, losing more altitude. Dawn was now breaking slowly. Actually they had covered quite a bit of distance, Buddy had a thought in the back of his mind if they could make it to that area they went down before which would be kind of ironic, but there would be hope they could get some help there again. The bad thing was, he did not want to jeopardize the Frenchman for helping him the first time. Would he be able to bring this plane down that close this time would he actually be that lucky only time would tell, Things took a turn for the worst the engine that was running started to smoke. The plane shook violently. He knew it was time to figure on putting it down. While he still had some power. He didn't want to come in dead stick. He pulled the handle to let the landing gears down. Of course, nothing happened. Whether this was good or bad it made no difference. He was looking at the tree tops about right now, trying to see the best way to bring it in, hoping the ground was soft. Maybe they were lucky and the farmer had plowed the field, making it soft there for a belly landing he heard the radio come on the other plane was trying to reach help if there was anybody out there, the Hawk is going down. There was no answer back, unknown to them, the Germans had picked up this transmission and notified everyone that the Hawk, also known as the Yank was going down somewhere in their area. This would put the other plane in danger. A few more times he heard the radio again with no answer. By now, Buddy was hoping Teal would get out of there and head back there was nothing more they could do for him they needed to protect themselves. Although he knew Lieut. Teal would be able out fly most of those Germans that they would send up after him. Also hoping the Wolf wasn't in the area and heard this. Right now he really had to concentrate on what he was doing to bring this plane in or crash. To parachute out was not an answer, he wasn't sure Craig was dead. Just then his engine stalled. No time to restart then flaps down trying to bring the nose up so he wouldn't slam hard into the ground nose first. Thankfully the nose did come up slightly but then there was contact with the ground crunching grinding Buddy was being thrown around inside the cockpit. Even though he was strapped in, it felt like his shoulder was being torn away from his body, low tree branches crashed against the canopy popping it right off. There was a loud smack against the side of his head then something hit his chest. The plane finally came to a screeching stop with a cloud of dust and dirt, smoke and fire followed this, then there was peaceful, quietness.

There were short periods of consciousness racked with pain, labored breathing, along with whiteness again. Then another awakening with the thought in Buddy's head, he had to get Craig and himself out of this plane. It was on fire they would both die, then that blanket of unconsciousness would come over him again. Buddy felt strong hands on him, pulling lifting, carrying, he felt the heat against his face half in, half out of a conscious state. Wondering if it was Craig doing this, somehow, he knew it wasn't for one thing, Craig wasn't that big of a man to do this also for a second or two opening his eyes he saw someone slumped over in the back of the cockpit knowing it was Craig the plane fully engulfed in flames, his leather jacket with the star patch on the shoulder laying in his front seat then blackness again.

Jacque, the French farmer as usual was up early before daylight, rambling around the kitchen, making himself breakfast. When his daughter Janelle came in to finish, giving her a smile. She was a striking girl raven black hair with white complexion. These days, she would dress with sloppy clothing attempting to hide her body from the prying eyes of some very rude soldiers she was always leery of them she normally had a very warm personality except for the despairing look in her eyes because of what had happened to her country. Her mother had died years ago her father had raised her well. The hard work on the farm had given her unusual strength for her size, her father a huge man with large hands of course working on a farm, always created hard physical work, giving him incredible strength.

As he finished his breakfast looking out at his farm he could see daylight beginning. Wondering what this day would bring. He could hear what sounded like motors of airplanes fairly close to the trees not far from the farm house also there came, loud screeching grinding noise. He could see the plane had plowed into the ground and hit one of his Apple trees, the plane looked like it was on fire,

He grabbed his hat, running out the door down to where the plane was on fire. He noticed one of the wings was on the ground flames were engulfing the area near the cockpit realizing this was a British plane because of the insignia on the side. There were two men inside. He quickly unbuckled the man in the front seat grabbing and pulling him out up into his arms as he walked down off the wing, he was moaning, seemed to be unconscious. He raced back up the wing then grabbed the other man in the back the flames were really high he reached down to unbuckled, but was having trouble then noticed part of his side was gone. Laying his fingers against his neck the man had no pulse then a loud pop as flames started to burn out of control. He had to leave the man there. Janelle had raced down to the plane, saw a man laying there then yelled something in French for her father to get away from there, it's going to explode. So he proceeded down off the wing grabbing the man off the ground, trying to be gentle if possible. They both scurry up toward the chicken coop, where they knowingly had a place to hide him under the boards of this building. She slid the boards aside, attended to some of his wounds that need to be taken care of immediately, then shoving the torn and bloody clothing under the boards, laid him down on top of them, She checked his pulse again he was still alive Jacque hesitated for a second looking at the Pilot, he recognized him from before also wearing that red scarf realizing this man was an American, sliding the boards back over top of him spreading the straw back over, like nothing had ever been moved. They quickly went back to the house then they heard a loud explosion. He told her to stay where she was, as he proceeded back toward the fire. Knowing the German patrols would soon be there, surprising that they weren't there already. He wanted to act like he was on his way down to that area. Now it was total daylight very soon the area became surrounded by German soldiers, asking questions. Jacque tried in French to tell them what he had seen then he made a motion about the explosion. Still no one could get near the wreckage it was still in flames too hot to go near, after the questions stopped. He pardoned himself. They seem to understand as he headed into the barn then with a basket he went into the chicken coop to gather eggs as he did everyday. No one watching him he moved the board aside reaching down to touch the side of his neck. He could still feel a pulse then purposely walk around where they could see him then back to the farmhouse with the eggs. Some soldiers searched the barn, chicken coup also, the house and grounds through the trees to see if there was any evidence of another person that had tried to escape. They could clearly see the one body hanging outside the side of the fuselage being burned beyond recognition by now. They questioned him more. One of the soldiers could speak some French but very limited. They didn't quite trust him. But then again, they had to. He had helped a high-ranking German pilot once that had crashed near his farm also between him and his daughter they had patched him up well enough to get him to proper care and they were never to be touched by his order. This would help throw suspicion away from them in order to do their underground work which was far more important. Janelle's mother was a nurse in Italy before her family had moved to France. She had worked in several hospitals, so she had showed her daughter how to dress wounds and take care of people. Naturally, she did not do her best with the wounded or hurt Germans she would fix them up just enough to keep them alive, maybe. Jacque had learned some German, which helped if they wanted to listen in on somebody's conversation. Of course, he never let them know. He was wondering why all the commotion about this one plane a lot more soldiers showed up, even some officers, he managed to catch a few words when the officers were speaking to the soldiers, one word was the American or the Yank, which meant the pilot. He put it together because he knew the patch on his shoulder was American, the same one that had came down before this was totally ironic and again they went over every piece of the barn chicken coop, house. They searched everywhere, even sent men away from the farmhouse in a circular fashion. Of course, he played dumb of it all, acted like he was confused. Some of the Germans even laughed about it, as far as they were concerned he was just some stupid farmer, that suited him just fine. After the main search party had moved away from the area, leaving three soldiers guarding wreckage Jacque carrying a bucket of water to the chickens as he usually did. After entering the coop the guards were unable to see him, he took a small rag moistened with water move the boards just enough to reached down, squeezing a few drops of water in the man's mouth, who was still unconscious, but alive, quickly replacing the boards spreading straw again as he walked back towards the house the guards seemed more interested in their own conversation, then what he was doing. Late that afternoon, the fire at the wreckage had smoldered down to almost nothing. The body by now was lying on the ground beside the wreckage Janelle and her father wished they could do something about burying him, but didn't dare to go near it. Some time later a truck pulled up near the body. The guards had a conversation with whoever was driving the truck as they watched the team put the body on a stretcher covered him with some kind of blanket. Then placing him in the truck they left headed for town. That evening after dark, the guards had built themselves a fire Janelle and her father decided to get some rest, still worrying about the man in the chicken coop. They were unable to do anything right now. Early the next morning before daylight he got up and looked down where there was only one guard standing there by the fire actually facing away from the house the other two soldiers must have had some place to sleep, so he dressed in dark clothing motioned for his daughter to do the same. The two of them slipped quietly around the barn into the coop, trying not to disturb the chickens, removing the boards with a very dim light she quickly redressed some of his wounds giving him more water while Jacque watched for any change by the fire.

With that accomplished, they slip back into the house quietly. After doing their early morning chores the farmer decided he better go to town as he normally did on this day not to arouse any suspicion. She would stay and take care of things and possibly have a minute to check if he was still okay, so Jacque went out to the truck trying to start it, after a few minutes along with a few tries the engine coughed a couple times then finally started, he slowly ambled the truck toward town, worrying about his daughter being left there he didn't trust any of the soldiers. A considerable amount of time had passed since the truck had left, the three soldiers still guarding the plane for what reason they did not know when one of them motion toward the sky as the sound of plane approaching all three took cover, with their guns pointed in the direction of the plane preparing to shoot if it wasn't one of theirs. Then they realized it was an FW one of their fighters, rather shiny after circling several times it landed, not far from the wreckage. One of the soldiers approached the plane that landed recognizing the pilot snap to attention also the other two following suit. The canopy open the person jumped down off the plane. This was a colonel, I am Wolfgang. The soldiers had somehow heard about him. They were a bit uneasy knowing his reputation. The conversation with the guards something to the effect of what happened to the persons in the plane. The guard explained about the truck that had come to pick up the body, Wolf said only one, yes sir said the ranking guard Wolf proceeded to look around the aircraft actually trying to get up inside then found what was part of a burnt leather jacket It had the insignia of the American patch partially visible. He had another conversation with soldiers they mention how they had searched the whole area for anyone else and found nothing. Not satisfied with what he heard he picked up a stick and start poking around the debris all around the outside of the aircraft several times looked around the bushes and trees, then into the barn and the chicken coop area spending quite a bit off time there banging, kicking moving stuff, had the guards helping him trying to pull up on some boards in the floor of the barn and following him to the coup, stomping, moving the chickens all away as they clucked in loud protest, knocking down some the roosts with the stick some of the egg smashing on the floor, then stomped out headed for the house motion for the guards to stay outside while he went in slamming the door open. Janelle was kind of in the doorway of the kitchen and sitting room. He brushed past her. She stayed as far away from him as she could in the sitting room. Jacque had done several of his normal errands, ending up at the general store. The man that he knew was one of them that also could help him, the store keeper Charles that had a list of things Jacque needed. This all looks good. He said you gave me one too many of these items. This was a code between the two, meaning only one survivor as he put it underneath some of the things on the counter, meaning they had hid one person. Reaching in the candy jar he brought out several pieces, one was broken. He put one back, meaning one person was dead the other was hurt it would take a while for him to heal. Jacque got the receipt back from Charles and borrowed his pencil then drew a star on the back the paper. The storekeeper looked around the store, making sure nobody could hear him then whispered really low "American"? The farmer shook his head yes the storekeeper nodded back. With that all done Jacque started up his truck and headed back to the farm. Wolf was more or less satisfied that he couldn't find anything in the house. The girl stood there watching him. She tried to cover herself, but he knew better. He would certainly like to have his way with her but it seemed like every time her father was there. This time she was alone Wolf advanced toward her as she back into the corner of the room. He took his jacket and scarf off, dropping them to the floor she tried to evade him, but Wolf was not having any of this, he grabbed her she struggled hard against him, but he was much more powerful he pushed her down on the couch pulling at her clothing. She kicked at him. He was stunned for a moment she was a lot stronger than was expected, he enjoyed this kind reaction, but then gained the upper hand momentarily, suddenly he was being literally picked up and thrown against the wall where he fell to the floor, disoriented for a second, he looked up and saw this giant of a man standing over top of him, Wolf, had a very strange expression he couldn't believe what had just happened. Realizing there was no way he could go up against this man. He scrambled over toward the wall where he had dropped his gun belt, withdrew the pistol from the holster pulling the hammer back pointing it at the girl's father. The large man stood his ground actually moved closer, staring in Wolf's eyes never flinching with his daughter behind him, daring him to pull the trigger. Just about that time, the two soldiers that had been outside, stepped into the room to see what the commotion was all about. There was a very tense moment the gun did not scare Jacque. Had Wolf pulled the trigger and shot him, this would have given this huge man an excuse to tear this Nazi pig to pieces there was no doubting that. However, the tense moment came and left Wolf holstered the gun, retrieved his scarf, jacket then straightened up his clothes, stomped out of the house heading back to his plane, the soldiers following him Janelle rushed to her bedroom. It wasn't long before everyone heard the plane startup and take off. There was kind of a big sigh of relief after the noise of the engine faded away to quietness. After a few minutes Jacque went to Janelle's room, by now she was mad and enraged more then crying. She looked at her father with appreciation.

CHAPTER TEN

Jacque realized a few hours later the guards were gone, as he had been doing his chores. He heard a vehicle pull up near the wreckage, then leave. He still did not want to take any chances the rest of the day both, he and his daughter were watching all around the farm, making sure no one was still lingering around, several times cautiously he would check on the young man and was satisfied that he was still alive. They both decided to wait till nightfall to get him into the house. Much later outside listening intensely for some noise, with a very dim light Jacque was able to pick him up as gently as he could taking him into the house, she rearranged the chicken coop to look normal, in the house they had left a small light on with the heavy drapes closed so no one could see inside. Janelle had previously prepared hot water and bandages to be ready. She had mixed a few things together as her mother had taught her to make a solution to help heal open wounds. After being laid on a blanket they quickly disrobed him modesty at this point was not an option. She went to work on him, cleaning, putting bandages made out of torn cloth back on him. There was a severe gash across the side of his head, along with other places on his body. He had a broken arm. His leg was damaged, along with a few broken ribs, bruising, on the side of his chest. The farmer had left the room while his daughter was taking care of the young man, he went to the kitchen, also walking around out side listening. In the meantime, she had straightened his arm, putting on a splint. He moaned several times. She knew it was very painful, but had to be done. She had wrapped some material tightly around his chest to help with the broken ribs. He moaned some more. She put her two fingers on his lips to comfort him, hoping her touch would transmit to them that someone was taking care of his wounds. As she touched his mouth, something transmitted back to her, a feeling of trust.

It seemed very easy for her to sooth and touch this young man's body in spite of the traumatic experience she had experienced earlier she had never had any dealings with American men. She only knew that American men that were here fighting were volunteers which spoke for their character. She welcomed the chance to treat someone that was here maybe to help them get their country back from these men that controlled her country along with her friends. Right now she had more important things to take care of. While she feverishly worked on him she noticed his breathing became very shallow. He started to shake this really worried her. He was going into shock, which wasn't good. Then he relaxed too much and stopped breathing. Her fear was coming true. She put her lips on his and blew several times, then turned him on his side. She didn't dare to push on his chest because of his broken ribs. She heard him taken a breath of air. So she did that again. He eventually started breathing on his own. He started shivering almost uncontrollable. She knew his body temperature was dropping. She remembered what her mother taught her about transferring body heat from one person to another. Also she had read or heard the Germans in their sick way of experimenting with human bodies had proved this was the best way they found to bring someone's body heat back up, so she disrobed most of her clothing, pushing her body against his, while wrapped in a blanket. She held him tight to her, rubbing briskly on his skin with her hands against his back and neck trying to increase his circulation his breathing became steady, after several minutes, the shaking settled down. She held him a little while longer to make sure then slowly eased her body away from his realizing she had never felt the man's body against her this way. She smiled to herself as she got fully dressed again, a light knock at the door as her father entered the room. She smiled at him, which meant everything was okay. She had a short conversation, telling him what had happened. He had a real concern knowing she would do everything possible to help this young man stay alive. She was so much like her mother. They had made a small place behind the wall that was very secure and enough room where they were able to hide somebody, also work on their bandages. Buddy remembered the plane hitting the ground sliding crunching grinding noise. The canopy being knocked off, then total darkness. There were strong hands pulling lifting him up, then blackness again several times just semi-awareness feeling excruciating pain, then a musty smelling place with weird noises sounding like chickens clucking, once in a while there would be a welcome wetness against his mouth, also more pain. Feeling of soft hands on his body more periods of darkness, unable to open his eyes it was very dark, he could not take a deep breath because of the pain in his chest, then welcomed darkness where there was a lot less pain, he would feel those warm, soft hands on him again. It was a pleasant feeling through all the pain it almost reminded him of when he was younger getting hurt his mother would sooth him with her soft hands he knew he wasn't dreaming. Buddy struggled with consciousness at times, once in a while he heard voices it wasn't English. It was probably French. He was unable to understand. There seem to be long periods of dark quietness, then periods of activeness. This is when he struggled with staying conscious trying very hard to open his eyes and focus. It took him several times before he could accomplish this. At first it was just some blurred images then back to that dark fuzzy feeling. He wasn't sure how long he had been there, it seemed like awhile he couldn't tell if it was days or weeks finally during one time of consciousness he was actually able to open his eyes and focus what he saw was unexpected and pleasant, somewhat blurred. There was a round face with real dark hair and brown eyes, with a slight smile. He thought to himself so this is what Angels look like, he was trying to say something, but nothing came out of his of his mouth he tried to raise his arm it felt like a lead weight he decided not to do that then tried to speak again. He felt those warm fingers on his lips. Now he was able to put the fingers with a face. It was nice. Then felt that darkness come over him again and did not try to stop it, he kind of knew what was happening. It was easier to just let that be, rather than try to fight it.

It took time but they had fairly long periods of consciousness now she would feed him, mostly broth and soup. He tried several times to move his body, but was unable it seemed to create a lot of pain. She would look at him and shake her head no he thought to himself, I better listen to her. She would gently rub his arms. Also move them up and down slowly, watching his expressions. She did this several times a day along with his legs eventually he was able to do this on his own she would smile to see his progress. Naturally he would overdo it, the pain would start all she had to do was look at him then he knew he had done wrong again. From then on, he let her decide what was best for him.

He knew it had been about a week since he had gained full consciousness. There were times it was dark in the room he was in when she was there he could see a window in the hall outside this room sometimes the sun would shine in that was a nice sight. Every morning after she would feed him then she would start his exercise. This seemed to work really well. They started to communicate slowly by pointing at things and saying them in English then in French every once in a while they would have a problem understanding, all in all things moved along fairly fast. Buddy made motions over his head to the floor then pointing to himself trying to find out how long he had been there. It took several times she finally held up her hands and then one hand again meaning two weeks, give or take a day he was sure it wasn't that many weeks. They had to hurry sometimes to get him behind the wall into his little room when German patrols came through they would always check the house that was becoming less and less.

Her mother had left a lot of nursing equipment when she passed away Buddy was using a portable urinal one day when Janelle came into the room He tried to cover himself turning away from her. She quickly turned around, not to embarrass him. She thought to herself. This was very refreshing. She had several uncomfortable situations with some of the soldiers they would expose their selves while urinating, laughing at her. They were just plain crude.

Buddy knew that she had cleaned him at times he felt her hands on his body, but he still felt respect also not to openly flaunt himself, from then on she would knock first, then enter.

Jacque and Janelle tried to maintain their routine going about their daily chores things that needed to be done. Of coarse she did the most, taking care of Buddy. There were several times when her father would come in to check on his progress, he would smile then tap him on the shoulder shaking his head yes. By now she had learned quite a bit of English. Also teaching her dad some for now and future use. She was very proud of what she had done with this young man. She admired his well conditioned body along with his nice teeth, blue-eyed blonde hair he was very tall, but not as tall as her dad. The only thing that was really bothering her about everything was the red scarf. She recognized how close the match it was to the one the German officer was wearing. Even the color the tassels everything was the same. She had been taught at a young age how to repair clothing crochet, knit. So knowing it was handmade how did he have possession of this Scarlet Scarf another thing in the back of her mind how similar in looks these two men were even though the left side of his head was damaged she could tell however being very happy that's where the similarities stop this man was completely different in every way.

    By now she had been able to remove his splints from his leg and arm, even though his leg had not been broken. She wanted to protect it. He was able to stand now she had come up with a pair of crutches, so he was able to move around slowly gaining strength in his legs, bringing his muscles back to use he almost fell a couple times, she was right there to grab him, surprised at her strength they would smile when she grabbed him, he was quite a bit taller than she was but also able to handle him with ease.

    Janelle had altered some of her father's cloths to fit him while his clothing had been washed she was able to mend some of the torn pieces as best she could. Everything was put under the floorboards of the room one day Buddy asked her about the scarf. He made a motion around his neck. She knew what he meant as she pulled the floorboards apart bringing up his clothing along with the scarf she did notice he was not overly excited about the scarf. It seems like he just wanted to know where it was, satisfied he told her to go ahead and put them back. She was a little relieved at his reaction to the scarf

    Buddy wondered to himself, if his family also his mother knew what had happened. He knew she would be in a terrible state because of this, there's no way he could get in contact with anyone, he thought about the guys back at base, he felt really bad about Craig wondering if he could have done anything different to save him, knowing he had to let it go for now. He was just really glad that they had accomplished their mission that had been very important to a lot of men. If it had slowed down or stopped the production of the fuel for those jet planes. Sometimes trying to justify things is hard to accept. He also hoped Teal had made it back.

His leg had healed enough so one evening he was escorted out into the night air. He was very excited to be outside. He raised his arms high over his head both Janelle and her father were also very excited for him, Buddy almost lost his balance. She was right there to grab him also her father grabbed him to prevent him falling, those hands felt very familiar they were the ones that dragged him out of the burning airplane. Being able to smell the outside air, hear crickets chirping a light breeze, he was very thankful for all of this. He had always liked to be around farms, slightly remembering what it was like in Canada. He had thought many times after the service of having a farm working the land, growing things was a hard life but a very good life. No doubt in his mind. This is what he wanted when he got back home. Janelle and Buddy had grown very close to each other. It was hard to determine how their actual feelings were because they're spending so much time together. Plus, she nursed him back to health. A lot of men fall in love with nurses that take care of them this is just natural. Also they had no one else to communicate with except her dad so they were together a lot. She knew she had never met anybody like him when he touched her it was very gentle. He had a very caring way about him if she happened to drop something he would try to reach down to get it for her. If they were leaving the room he would reach over to grab the door to open it, these were qualities that proved what he was like when he smiled at her or did anything to help her. Her heart would start beating and she would have that feeling deep inside her. She wanted to be near him all the time. Deep inside she was worried because she knew she was falling in love with him. She was also worried maybe he didn't feel that way about her, but his actions, the way he treated her. She knew he had feelings for her more than just nursing. Buddy started having feelings deep inside him about this beautiful girl that was taking care of him. He wanted to be more than just a nurse and patient. Always wondered what woman he would ever consider spending his life with, the more he was around her the more he knew she would be like her. By now he knew the way she touched him. She had feelings also, whenever together. Sometimes they would be laughing fairly loud. Jacque would hear them laughing, it made his heart feel good to hear his daughter laughing, enjoying her life compared to what it had been up to now, but then he started to worry. Knowing in the future, things would have to change this young man would be healed up enough to leave to go back where he was stationed knowing he was an American also made things even more difficult for both of them. He also knew his daughter's was having deep feelings for this young man. One day while he and his daughter were talking he brought up the situation, warning her to try to check her emotions to realize the whole problem about him having to leave to go back. She knew her dad was right, but she also knew that by now things had progressed very far for the two of them, because a few days ago these things were on her mind while she was talking to Buddy when tears welled up in her eyes. He knew instantly what was happening took her in his arms holding her close, soothing her. Then he kissed her, both their hearts were beating fast. She made a sound deep in her throat. There were feelings deep inside her now awakening she had never felt before. Then he just held her for a long period of time. She knew then, somehow, someway, even though it was hardly feasible they would be together. He looked in her eyes and told her he wanted to marry her, holding her finger of the left hand, what ever it takes I will come for you after this war is over. Also your father, then half English half French he tried to tell her he had saved quite a bit of money sending it home to his mother with the intentions of buying a farm not far from where they lived, Janelle was getting very excited about the prospect of what could happen if this came true. Jacque standing on the porch looking across the fields that he had worked littered with airplanes, large pieces of metal and engines, holes in the ground thinking how would he ever be able to clear this wreckage to be able to farm again. His love for farming was diminished to almost an impossibility there would be no money to buy seed. Besides that there was an immediate threat to him and his daughter eventually being caught helping men like this They would both be immediately shot, he become very depressed, shaking his head he walked back in the kitchen, about then Janelle came into the room with a large smile on her face her eyes were happy. He did not want to depress her with his thoughts she started to inform him what had transpired in the room about what Buddy had told her he wanted to get married she was very excited about this trying to tell her father the way he had explained to her what he wanted to do for both of them. Her father listened intently, with some reservation. Not knowing what would be available if it was even possible to accomplish this. Jacque wasn't familiar with immigration. He knew a lot of his people in nearby communities had gone to Canada. However he had never thought about it he was happy and content where he was until now, for a few minutes he even experience excitement at the possibility of farming in that country but then, would there be any difference except for the language, farming no matter where would be basically the same. The other thing he was hoping this man would be true to his word, which so far he had been. He was an officer, a pilot also an American volunteer this had to carry some weight. Jacque also was worried even after the war was over if their lives would still be in danger knowing the Germans also how vindictive they were, would they still come after him and his daughter also other people that helped through the French underground. They would certainly blame people like us for helping them lose the war. Jacque had made several trips to town the last one he was able to notify the storekeeper the progress of our young pilot in that he was becoming much better, soon he would be able to travel maybe in about two weeks. If there was something coming up the storekeeper would send his son to deliver some goods to his farm and let them know. With that the farmer headed back toward his farm, not wanting to leave for very long at a time, in case the patrols would come back by the house he always wanted to be there. As he arrived back at the farm, Jacque went to the room proceeded to tell his daughter and Buddy about what she dreaded the most. Sometime shortly after next week it would be time for him to be transported. She wondered if he was ready for that, but it had to be, it was necessary for him to get back to recuperate. Maybe he can help with the effort to bring this war to an end. Janelle stayed in the room with Buddy to talk about what she had learned from her father. She had that look on her face. It was hard to hide, he tried to comfort her with his easy way, but he himself was having problems just thinking about having to say goodbye. So they would savor every minute they had together. He would do as much exercising as he could and try to build strength that he had lost, wondering to himself how this was all going to work, is he going to go back like he did before with the moon patrol also how would he get there, this would be interesting. After a week had passed they were notified that the moon patrol would be arriving the next evening, to have the man in the barn just before nightfall. Someone would come by in a wagon to take him to meet the moon patrol. Buddy was half excited, also sad at the same time, knowing he would not be flying soon. His condition would need a lot more work before he would be ready for any kind of activity like that, his leg had flared up again giving him considerable pain. The problem was there were no antibiotics to fight infection. She had done an excellent job with what she had to work with, making up solutions with what they had available. Now that they knew when this would happen their anxiety was very high. That evening she dressed his wounds also really worried if he was going to be able to make this trip. Then again, she knew he had to. He needed other medicine that she couldn't provide for him to heal. When she was done with the dressing she looked at him, trying to hold back tears. He put his fingers up to her lips to cover them like she had done to him she instantly had a smile on her face, as he took her in his arms and held her very close to him. Buddy never experienced these feelings. Of course, there was a certain love for his mother that was nothing like this. Because it went deep inside it's like something you have, but never want to let go, someone intimately close to you the rest of your life. He laid on the pad with the blanket, his arms around her. He knew he had a job to do when he was well enough, but no doubt in his mind this woman Janelle that was in his arms would have a big effect on his life in the future, these two people, along with others like them were very instrumental in helping soldiers like himself and others. They sacrifice their lives every day, every hour, every minute, why wouldn't there be a way to try repaying them somehow. These were simple people living a simple life but doing an amazing thing. Without them, he would be dead along with a lot of British, American, and with other allies. After Buddy had fallen asleep she eased her way from his arms and left the room. It was dark now, tomorrow night at this time if everything went right he would be gone. She was smiling because of his warm tenderness, also knew his love yet she had tears in her eyes. When she approached her father he knew this is what he had tried to warn her about. He was a large rugged man, but he sure had a soft spot in his heart for her. Janelle went outside, walked around for a while, trying to clear her mind. After about an hour she came back into the kitchen where her father was. She seemed to be a lot more at ease, Jacque wasn't sure what was going to happen when this was all over the circumstances were not in their favor. The only thing he knew for sure right now was his daughter's feelings with this young man. He took her by the arm down the hallway to the room where the young man was then opened the door lightly guided her in closing the door behind her. She knew as far as he was concerned she could stay there with him this night. Laying down on the pad with him her heart was beating fast he put his arm around her and pulled her close. Then she kissed him tenderly, he whispering things in her ear, outside of her father and mother this moment was the warmest safest place she had ever felt in her life. Buddy knew if he really wanted to right now he could have her. However, he wanted more than that he wanted a life with her and her father. Somehow he could see the future. Maybe it was wishful thinking it didn't matter. He felt in the future they would be on a farm somewhere not far from his family, would this be too much to dream for only time would tell. Janelle had given herself to him, but he didn't take advantage of it, she really respected him for that. Her love grew even deeper for him. Jacque turn the light out in the kitchen went out on the porch to his favorite chair just sat there listening, watching, he stayed awake that night, watching down the road listening for anything. He vowed this would be one night that his daughter would have peace in the arms of someone she loved. He was damn sure nothing was going to interrupt that. The next day things went fast, considering this was Buddies last day there, Jacque informed Buddy that he would bring his truck up to the back of the house to get some piece of machinery at that time they would sneak him in the cab then take him to the barn, a wagon would take him to meet the moon patrol. As the day progressed everything went as planned, just about nightfall two mules pulling a wagon came down the road, then into the barn were Buddy was hiding with Janelle, the crutches were replaced with a cane, there wouldn't be room for very much. She had packed him a small bag with food to have on the way also there was a bottle of water. Once the wagon had been unloaded then reloaded with manure, hay and straw. The seat was removed. After an emotional goodbye also a promises to Janelle and her father, Buddy crawled into the compartment. There was a canvas and a blanket for him. He struggled getting into a somewhat comfortable prone position still hurting catching his breath a couple times, the seat was reattached, the man driving the wagon smelled strongly of alcohol, but when he talked to, Janelle and her father in French his voice sounded fairly clear so maybe this was a way to draw suspicion away. As the wagon ambled down the road for some time the Frenchman would break out singing in a drunken fashion then voices could be heard that was German, Buddy could understand the difference now that he had learned some French language. Then there would be silence again for a while just the rumbling of the wagon going down the road. The man singing again it seemed like hours went by when you couldn't see anything. He knew he was in a lot of pain but then he was excited about the idea of being rescued, also about getting back to whatever was going to happen to him. He knew there would be a lot of rehabilitation, wondering to himself if they were going to send him back home to the states. He tried not to get too excited, that was a long ways off. The wagon finally came to a stop. There was an eerie silence for quite some time. Buddy was able to change his position it was a great relief also he was able to eat a little bit of what she had packed for him and drink some water, although it was dark he was able to manage this. He felt the bench move then there was a low voice. Something about, we are here now he had to stay where he was until the signal, no sense in taking any chances now. Buddy thought how amazing was the effort it took to accomplish this, but they had done this before. He had to salute each one of them for their courageous effort. More time passed, there was quietness in a distance was another sound coming at them. He hoped it wasn't a German patrol that's all they needed right now. The noise got very close to the wagon, it sounded like an engine of a truck. Then there were more voices that were in German. He could only think that there was another part of this scary plan for other men besides him then there was quiet again. The night air brought an inviting sound of an airplane but he can only assume this is what it was. This would be their way out. The engines grew closer you could tell as it came in and landed, cutting the engines back, then there were three loud taps on the side of the box. He struggled to get out, he was in pain, but excited, as the man helped him down from the wagon, almost falling. With the cane and the help of this man he was able to make it part way to the plane, where there was a ramp going up. There were other people moving toward the plane. The Frenchman yelled out something in French to the fact that this man is hurt, he needs help. Buddy felt hands trying to help him up. He yelled back to the Frenchman thank you in French as he entered the plane and slumped against the side and slid down, laying there with pain racking his body. He felt the plane revving up, then bumping along the field then they were in the air someone with a thick British accent said are you okay mate. Yes, I think I am he replied. The voice came back saying you are American, Buddy answered yes, I am. Then someone said, I remember him. He was in our prison. He's the Yank that stood up to the Wolf. There was quite a bit of excitement throughout the plane over the roar of the engines. Several men pull their jackets off and put them under him, one for a pillow the other to protect his side. Someone said this is great. The Hawk is alive. Someone said he was missing in action or maybe dead. The next thing Buddy felt was the plane landing he could not believe that he was back in England being put on a stretcher then carried out of the plane. Now more than ever he would be able to finish what he had started. Thanks to all the people that helped him. He had more reason now than ever, a certain girl he loved then had to leave behind.

CHAPTER ELEVEN

Several days went by while he struggled to exercise, trying to get his limbs back in shape. He was up and walking, which was a big plus. His other wounds were healing, as was expected. The hospital staff worked on his side that had been injured. The therapist that was helping Buddy with his damaged leg was doing the same basic therapy that Janelle did for him back in France without her help He had his doubts if he would've made it to the plane. Every time he thought about her. He got that warm feeling deep inside. Early one morning, a captain came to him wanting to ask questions so they went to a private room where the captain did some debriefing Buddy knew he was from intelligence. He wanted to know some of the details of who helped him, how he was able to survive the crash also able to get to the plane to get back, Buddy gave him as much information as he could, of course, leaving out details of his involvement with Janelle, he did not think this was necessary. Also went on to explain to the captain how bad he felt about the loss of Craig, the captain tried to console Buddy by informing him that Craig had grown up in an orphanage. The service was his only life he would always take this kind of mission knowing other men had families and loved ones, he would always volunteer also one of the best navigators. Craig would be given a medal for his contribution. He was also giving some of his money to the orphanage where he grew up. Buddy made a note of that, he would certainly do the same. He asked the captain, have my people been notified of this situation the captain informed Buddy that everyone had been notified, including his family, also the men at his base. The captain also told him he would be eventually transported to the states for recuperation. He was excited about this news. About two weeks later Buddy was resting after his therapy he looked toward the door, there were a couple of smiling faces looking at him one was Whip's the other was Dean, also Teal along with a couple other guys that he had been flying with. It was a happy reunion handshakes tapping on the arm, shoulder, Whip grabbed his bad arm not knowing. Buddy kind of caught his breath for a second Whip quickly apologized not knowing it was his bad arm. He told his friend that was the best damn pain I've felt in a long time they all laughed glad that he was okay. They managed to get him in a uniform then took him off the base to a local pub where the guys drank some beer while he drank coffee. They talked laughed and joked it was the best time he had since he could remember .Eventually the topic of Wolf also the jet fighter came up, he had only been seen in Germany word came down that he had been severely reprimanded for taking the plane out of Germany into France. It seemed like they're keeping a close eye on him. However, he was still raising havoc with the bombers. But there had been a lot less use of the jet fighters. It seems like they were having trouble getting fuel for them, somehow, someone had exploded a few bombs at the fuel production plant also the rail system there. We wonder who really did that. There were quite a few smiling faces around the table, Buddy made a comment to the effect of a life sacrificed to save other lives. There was a toast to Greg and moment of silence. The day grew to an end they decided to take him back to the base when Buddy rose to his feet he winced a little bit. It took him a minute to move, they had been setting for quite a while, Whip looked at him and said you're moving like an old man now. His reply was, a few more crashes like that one then I will be an old man, lots of laughter. After getting him back to the barracks. It was somewhat of an emotional goodbye knowing they would not see him for quite some time. One day not long after his visit with the guys. He was surprised with the visit from Maj. Morrison and Capt. Harrison. They came by to see how he was doing. Also, to inform him how they were going to send him back to the states, Maj. Morrison did have a couple questions for him being in intelligence. He wanted to know some of the details. Buddy was more than glad to tell him, he knew that information would be safe with this man. He thanked them both for coming, by the way, the captain said your family will be glad to see you, Buddy smiled with appreciation. After a week went by he was strong enough to get on a plane headed for the states his excitement level was really high who wouldn't be. Paula was very surprised when both her brother and CT showed up showed up at her place with smiles on their faces, telling her that Buddy had been rescued. She instantly broke out in tears of joy she grabbed both CT and her brother with a big hug. Of course, they had been informed of Buddy's missing in action, sketchy reports would come through once in a while but nothing definite, even for CT with his contacts through intelligence reports were not really clear. The one good thing was no death notice. This was most encouraging news. Certainly she was beside herself with anticipation and concern, not knowing that was the biggest problem, her days and nights became a blur of concern. Every time CT would call the first words out of his mouth was about Buddy, with no news sometimes was good news. When she heard that he was back in England, also hospitalized she had extreme relief, now knowing that he was coming home. She was beside herself with excitement, but had to understand that he was still in a convalescence state. Once the plane landed, it seemed like it took forever to taxi and the engines to shut down. They had been able to fly right to the Curtis plant which now was a training base attached to an airport. Buddy with the help of a couple guys made it off the plane he touched the ground and thought it's good to be home. Then he was engulfed in a pair of arms around him. There's no doubt in his mind that was his mother. Then he saw his uncle Jim smiling shaking his hand with a one armed hug It was a little hard walking with his mother wrapped around him tears were streaming down her cheek. Buddy was glad she had not seen him before in his worst state. Tim had made sure they had the car there for him and took him to base operation CT grabbed Buddy by the shoulder and shook his hand, saying he was glad to have him back. Also, we have a lot of catching up to do all three men knew exactly what he meant by that. But there would be plenty of time for that later. CT informed Buddy to check into the hospital much to Paula's insisting she could take care of him herself, but then had to realize he still belonged to the military. After several hours of all this, they ended up at Jim's house, the two children Roy and Nancy were very excited to see Buddy, they stood at attention and saluted, then ran to him lightly hugging his legs. They had been told about his injuries, curious to know how it had happened, was he going to be okay, as he sat down in the chair, both the children reached up cautiously pointed at his medals, your a real hero aren't you, Buddy said he was not a real hero, they give you these medals because you do a good job. The boy spoke up and said, are you a real ace pilot, Buddy replied I guess I am. But there's a lot of men like this where I come from. He got emotional loving every second of being with these children this was what it's all about, protecting them along with the rest of the people here at home from those atrocities the evilness with what the Nazis were doing to the people they had under their control, the evilness was unbelievable, but true. He was more determined than ever to get well enough to go back and pick up where he left off. Things were certainly going in their favor. Now the Germans were backing off on all fronts. Paula and Nonny had prepared a great meal for everyone to celebrate Buddy's return. Of course, Paula took every opportunity to hug on her son, Nonny wanted to wait on him no matter what he wanted, so they all sat down to a great meal with lots of easy talk. No one really wanted to get into a serious conversation to start with CT, Jim and Buddy of course talked airplanes, engines also flying. Buddy congratulated CT on his promotion to a Full Bird Colonel, which it happen some time ago, he certainly deserved it .Then Paula had several questions about how he had been hurt, who had taking care of him, also were had he been that he was unable to get word out. He tried very hard to answer her questions as best as he could, not able to give her details. He did not want her to have certain information also didn't want her to know what he had gone through. She would only fret more about that. Buddy made light on the situation they had experienced only telling her he was well taken care of by a French family he explained that all the things the French people had worked for had been taken from them, any medicines or anything like that to be used on German soldiers that was the way things were in a war. Paula spoke up saying they had been notified that he was missing in action then they were notified again when he was back in England. She looked at CT, knowing he was the first with the information Buddy smiled, it's nice to have certain people around with certain information. Yes it is. She said as she reached over and kissed CT. The evening came to an end with Buddy having to leave with CT to go to the hospital, where he would start his rehabilitation, Paula still saying she could take better care of him then any hospital everybody agreed, but rules are rules. So reluctantly, she let him go after a big hug from her along with all of them. As CT drove to the hospital Buddy was staring long, hard out the window. CT asked is it good to be back? He answered I see all of this, the peace and quiet here compared to what I saw in England with all the devastation, the bombings, people dying. My heart goes out to that struggling nation. If people would've seen what I saw, they would have been involved in this war a long time ago, however we are in it now, I must say things are changing for the better. CT went on to say, you Jim and I with have some serious things to talk about. We have something big that we are working on you will be part of it. Buddy got excited. However, he knew CT wouldn't tell him about it yet. He had already been checked into the hospital. So he went straight to his room. It had been a long day, he was tired. He wanted to get some good rest he had a lot on his plate for tomorrow, the next day also from then on it was going to be hard work with pain until he got better. He was sure looking forward to being well again. Buddy started his exercises with a bang. His physical therapist Sam had been a football player while going to college to become a doctor, but decided he didn't want to go to school for that long, so he settled for physical therapy. While playing football He had been hurt, after going to several different therapists gaining nothing. He decided to do his own work coming up with a routine to help build muscles, so he started working on Buddy everyday, they also did other exercises to, Sam had never met anyone like him, knowing this man was determined to get back on his feet. So he did everything he could to help Buddy. It was almost unbearable at times, but he hung in there gritting his teeth bearing the pain getting stronger every day ever once in a while he would smile to himself, his heart would be warm. He would think about Janelle and her father, two very important people in his life, he had to get better so he could get back to them he just wanted to put his arms around her and hold her close. Yes, he pushed himself far beyond expectations every weekend he would stay with either his uncle Jim or his mother, who definitely wanted to take him home with her, but he wasn't in the mood to be sheltered. He loved his mother but that wasn't part of his routine. She would joke with him that there was something more pleasant there at the hospital then at her house, smiling. Buddy would just tell her no, just pain. She never could quite understand that. Then sometimes on weekends he would stay with his mom letting her pamper him that would always make her feel good. Of course, he had to visit Nonny and the two children. His mother had noticed how he had changed mentally he wasn't the same young men that had left. He had a different outlook on life now he had grown-up. There were times when CT Jim and Buddy had long meetings. A lot of it was about the jet fighter trying to figure out its weaknesses, how to approach taking them down when possible. That's where Buddy's experience came in, especially if flying the Spitfire he was able to get off a few rounds against that jet fighter that was interesting to CT and Jim While they were designing other planes with that in mind, how to make a plane that would be able to even come close to that. Buddy was told that they had been working on something not quite as fast, but a very excellent plane, it had been in the experimental stage for quite some time, but now they had stumbled onto something extraordinary and had started production, as soon as he was ready Buddy would be right in line for this. Several months went by Buddy was healing extremely well also responded to therapy above and beyond. He started out jogging, slowly working up more and more every day. He was basically done with his therapy he thanked Sam for his help, without him, his rehabilitation wouldn't have been this fast. He could now just concentrate on his running.Paula then informed Buddy that she was throwing a big party for him that she was inviting a lot of his friends from school that were still here, not overseas somewhere or had moved away . She especially invited some of the girls he used to go out with that were still single. Buddy was excited to see all of them. They all realized everyone had grown-up, things were little a different now than when they first got out of school. Pearl Harbor was still fresh in their minds, things had changed this country had gone to a war machine. The same thing was on all their minds, but they were really happy to enjoy the company of Buddy's caliber, especially the girls .His mother was hoping he would connect with one of them. The party was a great success. Everyone really had a good time, but to Paula's surprise. Her son didn't seem to carry on any serious conversations or ask any of the girls out on a date. Even though there were plenty of offers. He just remained calm, enjoyed visiting and thanked everybody for their company. This bothered her for a while, she asked Jim and CT if they knew if there was something wrong with her son, not wanting to get involved with any of the girls, was it because of the work or had something happen to him. Neither one of them had an answer. CT did mention the fact that somebody had helped him when he was in France. He knew it was a female and her father. He told Paula that every time Buddy would talk about her. He did seem to get emotional, so there might be something there. CT could not say too much, even though he knew more. Finally, one evening, she sat down with her son asking is there a reason why he didn't want to get involved with any of the girls here in his hometown. Buddy took quite a while to answer the question. Then he started telling his mother about what had happened that he felt very strong about the girl that had helped him possibly saved his life. Paula realized how serious Buddy was about her she asked him do you think you are in love with her. His reply was I know I've never had these feelings before, I know it's not because she nursed me back to health, but I have this feeling when I'm with her the tenderness I've never felt like that ever. He told his mother I hope you understand what I'm saying I am going to do everything in my power to help her and her father to be able to come here if everything works out all right. I'm sorry I haven't told you this before, but there's a reason why I can't. You will have to trust me, these people lay their lives on the line every day to help people that are injured or have to escape if the Nazis ever get a hold of this information they would kill them immediately. You don't know what it's like over there, how they live or what they do for people, so trust me when I tell you I can't say a lot, also I need you to not reveal this information to anyone. Will you do that for me, she was quiet for a few minutes, absorbing all of this then she said to him, yes, this is safe with me. Buddy asked Jim, how his mother and CT were doing Jim replied, basically the same as before she still had that problem. They both admired CT for hanging in there. You could tell they were very close to each other. He knew what it was like to feel that close to someone but not be intimate with them. Not long after that CT had Buddy up flying again. It felt good to be in a plane, he took it slow for a while then he started to push it. This was a P 47 that was used for training it was a good way to get him back up flying. One day after he had landed Jim and CT met him. CT said do you remember I told you we had something lined up,

Buddy replied, I'm ready for whatever you have for me, as they walked into the hangar CT said, this is it a P 51 Mustang a joint effort between the British and Americans with the Rolls-Royce engine in our plane. This is what we think is above and beyond any fighter plane out there. It may not be as fast as the jet, but it will out maneuver it, this has a very long range. So starting tomorrow, we think you're ready for this, Buddy said somehow I agree with a huge smile on his face. I just hope I'll be able to sleep tonight. Jim said if you want to, you can sleep in the cockpit. I engineered it for comfort Buddy said don't tempt me. All three of them laughed, knowing he was almost serious. Buddy was there early the next morning they opened the hangar doors. He fired up the engine you could feel the power Jim told him earlier to take it up and play with it for a while get used to the handling then start pushing it as hard as you can. It'll take whatever you throw at it. That is exactly what he did. He pushed the plane very hard, the power, speed, handling also maneuvering ability was amazing after about an hour of this he brought the plane back to the hangar. As you can imagine by the smile on my face that plane is awesome. The power even at higher altitude was above anything he had flown before, including the Spitfire now up against the jet fighter. He told Jim and CT, the speed was the only advantage the jet plane had over the P 51, but if you had two or three of these after one of those jets, he might make a mistake then you would have him. Buddy explained the weakness and how he had managed to shoot at it when it was vulnerable. It would be a very hard decision to make, stay with the bombers or go after that fighter plane. After the meeting was over Buddy went back to exercising, realizing how the G forces had affected his muscles he felt he needed to loosen up. He remembered also telling Jim and CT. It's one thing to be up there flying by yourself. But then, it's another thing to be flying against somebody with a similar plane you better know what you're up against both Jim and CT kind of had a smile on their face Buddy realize they were up to something he probably knew what it was. About a week later he was told to report to the hangar and there stood Jim and CT with 2 P51 Mustangs, Buddy knew right away what this was going to be. They suited up and crawl into their individual planes taxiing out headed down the runway. Once airborne CT took the lead Buddy was the chase plane. Mounted cameras in both planes to record everything that happened, they certainly weren't using live ammunition. It was a real battle between the two of them. This wasn't a friend against friend. This was plane against plane, pilot against pilot they really needed to know what real good pilots were capable of with this new plane. After a period of time it was his turn to be chased. Jim stood there watching for about an hour. It was an amazing battle between these two men he had to admit he could not tell who was a better pilot. They both came back and landed. Then, after exiting the plane's talking to Jim, CT said you have learned well. Haven't you, I could probably learn something from you. Buddy said, to Ct I have been in combat. That gives me the edge. It's different when you're up there fighting for your life, but everything I learned from you helped me in every way. The things you taught me, I just expanded on them, also a few tricks of my own. I learned with some pretty good pilots over there, they have to be, or else there not there anymore. Even the best of pilots are sometimes in a situation they can't get out of CT said, you mean something like an outside loop, Buddy looked at him with surprise you taught me that one don't you remember. So you heard about that CT replied back. It's nice to have perks being in intelligence Jim was beside himself with pride of this young man that he had helped raise also his accomplishments. Buddy turned to Jim you have built a magnificent war machine here. We have really needed this especially something that can go the distance to protect those bombers. This is amazing. I'm proud to be an American. CT was near the end with a class of cadets, teaching them as he had taught many other young men to fly, the class for that day was to watch some aerial combat between two pilots, their graduation day was next week, Buddy, had a chance several times to speak to the class. They were certainly taken with him, knowing he was what they call a double ace to them this was very impressive. However, he stood to the hard and fast rules of learning the art of flying. Several days later, Buddy was informed that he had to be in the parade along with the graduating class to have his uniform ready there were going to be a few Generals at this ceremony, so everything had to be spit and polished. Buddy was to lead the cadets on their march to the parade grounds, also to represent them. He was very proud to be part of the ceremonies. They all marched out to the parade field after naming off all the cadets they marched up individually got their wings with their promotions, with some pilot's receiving extra commendations for duties above their regular training then they returned back to their place in line. Then Buddy's name was called First Lieut. Williams, he snapped to attention and marched to the podium, wondering what this was all about. He was standing there in front of the Generals and CT, the General that was giving out all the wings and promotions started off saying by order of the United States Army Air Force, you are hereby promoted to the rank of Captain. The General handed him two clusters of silver bars then went on to say Furthermore, for your gallant effort, bravery, courage above and beyond the call of duty also never very from your steadfast approach to combat in the air also efforts to volunteer for dangerous missions beyond the call of duty, your accomplishments also the men you fly with hold you in high esteem. You have been awarded the Silver Star, the Purple Heart and the British Medal of courage this being forwarded to us from Air Marshal Ethan also Major Morrison and Capt. Harrison from your squadron in England. CT approached Buddy saluted him and pinned the medals on his chest then stepped back. Buddy still at attention snapped a salute the man returned the salute. He did an about-face marching back to take his place in line quite a bit prouder than when he went up there. There was a lot of applause hoops and hurrah's Buddy's thoughts went to the nightmares, the pain, the devastation he saw what he went through with the crash and the rehabilitation with more pain. But then it was all worth it to feel the emotion from all these people on his behalf, he only hoped that he deserved all this. Paula broke out in tears, trying to hold them back as much as she could, but with pride, joy and the love for her son. Jim was beside himself with pride. Also choking back tears, no father could ever be as proud then he was of his nephew, Capt. Williams. There were a lot of celebrations after the ceremonies. They all met at the officers club where they had dinner and drinks. Several of the young pilots came up and congratulated Buddy some of them being a little nervous just received their second Lt. bars, That was the lowest ranking officer, talking to a Capt. now, which was a bit intimidating, of course, Buddy didn't think so, to a point he had flown shoulder to shoulder wing to wing with a Sgt. pilot, but then realizing things were different here, you were an officer, and you had respect, this is the way it was, you had to accept that. Several other cadets had talked to him anybody knew right away these men were a little more sure of their self they were not cocky about it, but just confident about their flying ability. That was a big plus when you went up in a plane in combat. Of course, you have to be nervous, probably scared, but if you can settle into your plane and have confidence in your flying. It really helps one an awful lot CT had gave that to Buddy it seemed to work along with his calm, quiet nature. The dinner was going great Paula, Nonny and their friends all working together enjoying each other this was a night to relax even Buddy had a few drinks and loosened up at one point, the girls excused themselves to go to the restroom. Out of the clear blue sky CT and Jim asked him how good is Wolf? Buddy's eyes turned cold he got serious saying he's the best enemy pilot I have ever come up against, or that I know of from talking to other pilots. He's the best on their side. He has the fastest plane also he knows how to use it. He not only kills the plane, but tries to kill the pilots so thanks to your training along with the confidence also some of the tricks you showed me all paid off I was able to outdo him several times It's all because of your training I also learn tricks of my own. You have to in order to survive. CT said I would do anything to get into action. Buddy said. I bet you would, and you would be good, but you are doing the best thing for everyone. Right here right now, training these pilots to fly the best they can with what they have learned. You teach them teamwork, which is really important. Some of these men will owe their lives to you, no matter how good you are or how much you know there's always that unknown factor that will catch up to you. There's no training in the world that can protect you from that if you are in the wrong place at the wrong time you will go down maybe not from a pilot's guns, but I'm living proof there are other things out there that will bring you down. The girls finally returned, the conversation got a lot lighter Buddy said to CT and Jim, you both knew what was going to happen today, didn't you and neither one of you warned me about it one day I'll try to get even. Let's toast to all those behind the scenes, the quiet ones that help.

CHAPTER TWELVE

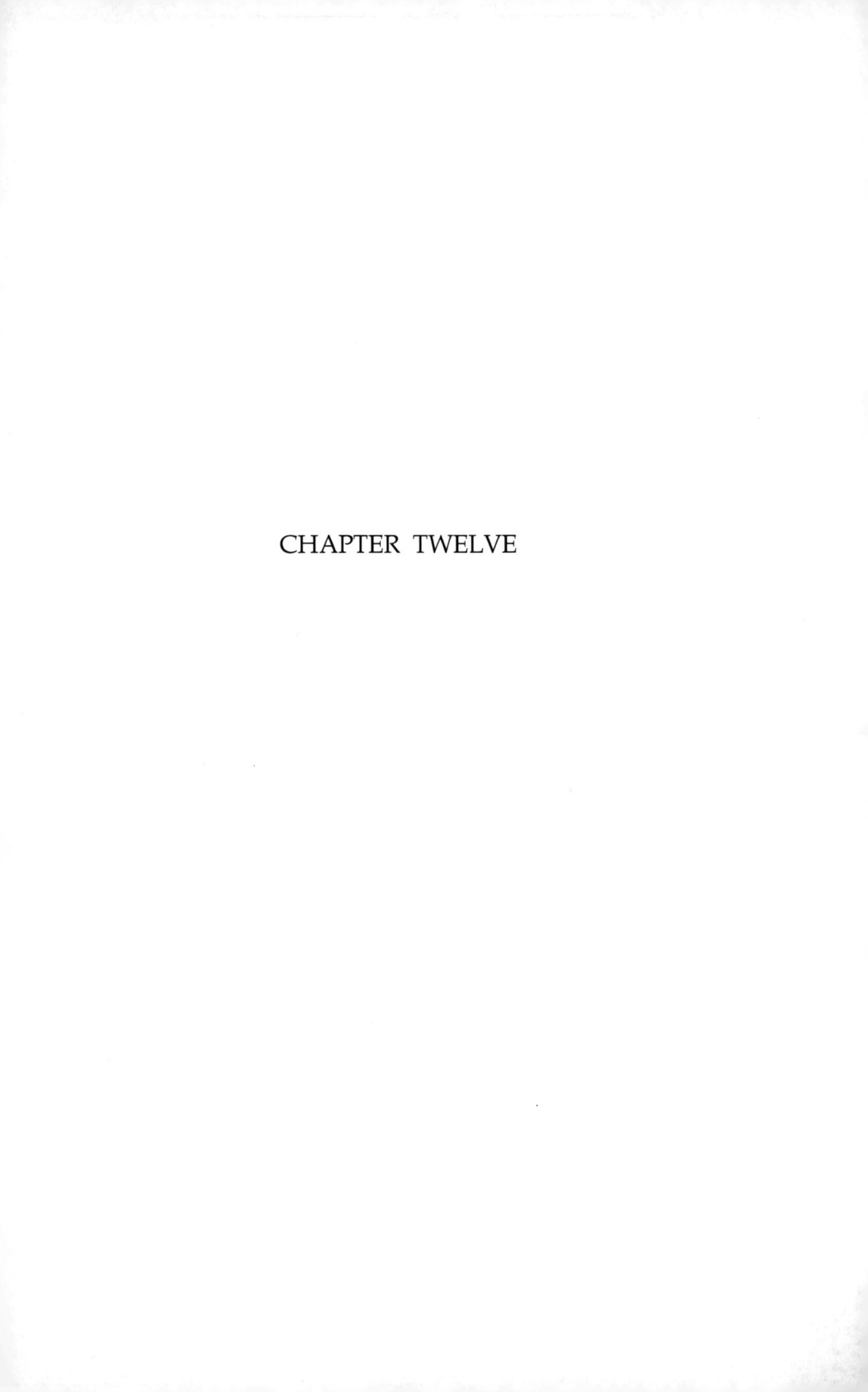

Buddy spent quite a bit of time with his mother along with his uncle and the rest of the family he knew it wouldn't be long before he would be leaving so he took every opportunity to spend time with them and the kids. It was Uncle Buddy, not cousin Buddy and he was fine with that. Every time he came to the house they would squeal and jump up-and-down run grabbing hold of his legs. They would hang onto him while he walked up the steps. Yes, this is what it was all about. A world away they were fighting a war, men, women, children dying bombs being dropped devastation it was hard to conceive this was even happening. Right now, all anyone could do is dream about having a family living here, maybe a farm not far away. Having children would this be too much to ask for. He hoped not. All good things must come to an end. Buddy was fit again in very good condition. He was ready. Actually, it was CT that gave him his orders. He was to be sent back to England to rejoin his squadron again. That was exciting for Buddy. He really liked flying with those guys. Well, now that you have your orders CT said, with your promotion along with that comes some responsibility. So follow me. They went out to the airstrip, there stood five P 51 Mustangs and four men, you will report to Maj. Morrison for more instructions. CT introduced Buddy to his men. This is Matt, Andy, Kyle and JR, they snapped to attention, recognizing these men from the class they were exceptional pilots in fact all four were at the top. CT said let's all relax for a minute. I need you to deploy within the next 48 hours. I'll give you an hour with your men and then meet me back at base operation. With that they all snapped to attention with a salute. Buddy felt a great sense of pride with his promotion also with responsibility to lead a group. He had the men relax for a while so they could talk, to get to know each other they seem to be at ease with him even though he was a captain. They had gotten to know him in their training class. JR spoke up saying we understand that you are the best pilot there ever was. Buddy replied back. I'm far from being the best pilot. Maybe I just got lucky, maybe in the right place at the right time. You also forget the man that trained you, he is the best. You never think your the best pilot also never let your guard down. The men who think that way things will always come right back around and bite you. Then Matt spoke up saying I know CT was a lot harder on me than the rest of the guys seems like everything I did he criticized, Buddy got a smile on his face he thought to himself, now where have I heard that before. On that note, he said tomorrow do whatever you have to do. I will check with CT and let you know exactly when we will leave, so have your bags packed and ready to go. With that they all snapped to attention then saluted, Buddy returned the salute then dismissed them he felt they were working as a team. He could feel it, this was a big plus .Buddy met CT back at base ops saying this was a surprise. I sure have had a few lately I appreciate the confidence you have in me, you know I'll do my best. Yes, CT said also that was your last surprise. I've hand-picked these four men to go with you. I expect you will get as much out of them as I have, especially Matt, but they'll listen well also toe the line. Buddy said I need to talk to you off the record for a few minutes, CT said I figured you would. I knew something was up. How about meeting me later at the officers club Buddy said that sounds great. Buddy had lunch with Paula and Nonny he told Paula to have Jim help her find a farm not far from this area and take the money he had been sending her to invest in the property. Nonny asked him, this seemed to be pretty serious I take it. I just hope and pray everything will work for you like it has for our family. We all love you and only want the best. We are very proud of you with what you have done we are kind of blind here of what goes on over there. I can't imagine what it would be like to have somebody bomb your cities killing people, including children it's hard for us to fathom some of those evil things. She got tears in her eyes. So did Paula. These tears were for people that are suffering. Sometimes you almost feel guilty, but we know you are doing the best you can, along with the other brave men that are fighting to keep the war away from us. Every night we pray for all of you and their families to. Buddy got all emotional about this. Sometimes we forget how our families back here cope with things they hear it's always good to know you are with us. Thank you, Paula asked when, do you think you will be leaving, he replied soon. With that he hugged them both. Telling them he would see them later. CT, Buddy, Jim sat down at the club, Buddy begins his story. He knew he could trust these men to keep this confidential He explained his feelings also wanted to know what it would take to get them over here after the war, which they agreed that it wouldn't be very long. CT said I will do everything in my power with my connections to do just that. I have a few favors owed to me I'm saving up, both in DC also in England. Of course you need to know these people also known as J an J, are always in danger of being caught, you know what happens if that does occur. Yes I realize the danger Buddy was shocked to know that CT had that kind of information. He shook his head in amazement then saying I also know it would take some paperwork with a lot of initiative on your part, if and when this all works out. You feel very strong about this young woman I can tell, this is not just some fairytale, having been around you enough to know how serious you are, Buddy commented her father also deserves a chance for what he has done to help both countries plus his own. He talked of his plans about the farm that Jim and Paula were going to take care of, excellent CT said to Jim if I can help in any way. I will, I'll do anything to spend time with your mother. They both smiled and laughed. Buddy said. Thank you for being there I know it's been hard on my mother with me over there, I know you've been there for her. I can't tell you how good that makes me feel. CT said well I won't see you again. I'm leaving. I have a special mission I'm taking care of personally before my next crew of Cadets start. He asked CT if there was anything he could say about it, all CT said was we're working on a nice basket of eggs for a city on the other side of the Pacific ocean Buddy smiled put my name on one of those eggs would you. CT said I will if you'll give a certain person a few extra shots for me. Buddy got a strange look on his face saying you know about it, what I'm trying to do. Yes, CT said we both want a piece of that shaggy dog. They both smiled and shook hands looking each other in the eye with mutual respect, goodbye good hunting, come back safe. That night they all missed CT at the big dinner that was set up for Buddy. It was lots of hugs, especially to the little ones, as they stood saluting, it was an emotional goodbye, Paula didn't want to let go of him. Excitement was the word of the day when Buddy and his four men took off, headed to England. The flight was long and quiet with lots of time to think. Also to check out the new fuel tanks designed for this plane to go long-distance and it sure worked for them while they flew. Of course, they had no ammo. That wouldn't be put on until we got ready to go into combat. As they got clearance to land, Buddy's excitement level rose to a high level as they landed then taxied to an area by the other planes. Buddy climbed out of the plane then immediately noticed that Axle was there to meet him as he climbed down off the plane he went straight to him stuck out his hand, Axle said. Welcome back stranger. The other four pilots join them just about then there were other guys there from the ground crew. What did you do bring me some new Cadillac planes I guess you're tired of our old jalopies. They both laughed, Buddy introduced the pilots to the ground crew telling them you better be nice to these guys because they are the ones that keep your planes flying in good order. So if you see them, when they're not on the flight line buy them a beer or a cigar if you see this man. He was referring to the crew chief who was chewing on a cigar. The four young pilots of course were used to spit polish snapping to attention, saluting, Buddy informed them things were a little less informal here compared to where you were, we all work together yes, we are still officers they are still enlisted men. However, we all have a job to do and standing at attention, saluting doesn't make the ground crew work any better on your plane. Axle made the comment that these Mustangs with that new Rolls-Royce engine that was quite a feat between our two countries, how does it feel to you, Buddy said it's an amazing plane also it can go the distance with the bombers and return with the auxiliary fuel tanks. It will out fly everything the Germans have out there maybe not as fast as the jet but very maneuverable and fast. Axle said this is exactly what we need to turn the tide. Even more, it's good to have you back, Capt. should I salute you twice Buddy said you better not have to do that with a smile. I'll check with you later. Buddy with his four pilots reported to Maj. Morrison, who was now Lt. Col Morrison, a well-deserved promotion, Col Morrison said what have you brought me Capt. Williams, the men snapped to attention as Buddy introduced them. The Col. told the men to stand easy, then saying, I guess you received our token of gratitude also your promotion extending his hand, you probably feel you didn't deserve it the way you think, but you along with several other men received the same medal, everyone did deserve it. Besides that look what this has brought us, your men with these Mustangs, which will be used to their fullest advantage. Things here have not changed very much. We are still losing planes every day, along with bombers, Capt., you with your men, along with other Mustangs, our hurricanes and spitfires will escort the bombers into Germany. The other planes will turn back to refuel while you're planes will go the distance. Then as you return our other fighters will be back up to assist. I can't tell you how excited we all are with this operation, along with our bombers also your Eighth Air Force bombers. We will be able to bring them to their knees soon. Also some confirmation on your behalf there has been a lot less activity from the jet fighters. It seems like they don't have the fuel to keep them all in the air as the Col. pointed to the metal on Buddy's chest. That's why you have that do I have to say anything more, saying this with a smile on his face. Also the next time you see a certain Col. Tom Gray give him my regards. You're dismissed. Buddy snapped to attention with the other four pilots, saying yes, sir, with a somewhat amazed look on his face on the comment about CT surprising how intelligence information works. The men gathered their bags along with Buddy then headed to the barracks where they were assigned their areas where they would be staying. He heard the planes returning. He also knew they would have to go through the debriefing he was really excited hoping to see most of the men he remembered. Then headed to the mess hall, everyone was very hungry by now, as they relaxed, settled into their meals, just about the time they finished the door flew open, income the pilots. Naturally when they saw Buddy It was hoops and hollers. Congratulation pats on the arms. Glad to have you back Capt, a lot of laughter with excitement in their voices wanting him to tell them all that had happened he felt great being back then, suddenly, he became a little worried. His heart sank a little he did not see his friend Whip. The door opened again in came Whip it was an emotional moment for both of them, Buddy said what's with the piece of cloth there Whip replied I brought this polishing rag because I heard you had two big heavy bars on your shoulders, so I thought I'd better bring this so I could polish them, for you, he said with a loud, Sir. They both cracked up laughing so did the other men. Besides that, you know, how hard it has been while you were gone keeping these guys in line while you were slacking and resting back in the states probably with sunshine and warm weather. Whip said good to have you back Capt. Buddy said I see you got your promotion. That's as high as you can go without being an officer, so when are you going to apply for officer school Whip replied I've had a hard enough time getting where I am now. I don't think I want to push it. Besides, too many officers now, my arm gets tired from saluting not only that, I see you brought me four more men I have to salute, more laughter throughout the building everybody enjoyed the banter between these two. Buddy introduced the four-men Whip was talking about. This is Matt Andy Kyle and JR, they had all been briefed on Sgt pilots how things were different here for pilots. Also, there were some faces missing among the pilots that he remembered sometimes it's better left unsaid.

At that time the door opened in came, flight Cmdr. Maj. Harrison as he came up, he and Buddy shook hands. Welcome Capt. It's good to have you back. I see you brought some heavyweights with you also some fresh pilots, nice medal there right, Buddy just smiled. Yes, I guess I do deserve this. The major said, we all need some sit down, talking to do. I want to know the details on your P 51's and what they are capable of. I know what information I have, however I need to hear from you what I can expect, then he was introduced to the four-men. After everything settled down somewhere toward evening, Buddy went to work out, he was glad to see they had expanded the workout room even more it seemed like a lot more men were taking advantage of that.

Briefing next morning was a somewhat different than before due to the use of the Mustangs. It changed how they would operate as they said they will meet up with other Mustangs to escort the bombers into Germany and back. After their meeting with flight Cmdr. Harrison, it was determined that was the best solution to utilize the distance of the Mustangs. After they were dismissed, Buddy assembled his group of men trying to make them understand the first combat flight was always the hardest. He also covered the fact that there were hunters and then there was the hunted that will come out later, after several combat flights. He informed Matt to be a leader just under him. The rest of the men understood. Once airborne, everything seemed to fall in place. The Mustangs with some of the spitfires went high. The other planes encompassed the bombers, just like before.

    Buddy would take turns using them as wingmen right now he had Andy with him. That would leave Matt in charge of two planes along with his own they would protect each other. Also, they were all lower, closer to the bombers. Then there were specs in the sky about their altitude Buddy called it in, everyone was ready he and Andy actually went higher trying to get a better jump on them. The first plane they went after was an FW after a few rounds went past the canopy of the FW it started doing maneuvers to evade them. Buddy with Andy stayed right with him and then he backed off calling Andy to come in. So he did, making several attempts to get in position also made several attempts to shoot at the FW, but missed he was being a little erratic with his plane, he seemed to have the advantage with the speed also maneuverability, but backed off a little when it came to shooting at him. Finally he did get a couple rounds into the German plane, but then backed off. Buddy saw this immediately went in to finish the FW, which was no match for the Mustang. Buddy had Andy rejoin the group then called Matt to join him.
    As they went after a couple other enemy planes he did the same thing with Matt, he went in to set up the attack. Matt seems to be much more aggressive about going in actually within a few maneuvers had the plane right in his sights, he seemed to be able to use the Mustang to its advantage. After several attempts he was able to get a couple rounds right into the plane staying right in there he was finally able to bring the plane down. That was number one for him Buddy could tell right away that Matt was a hunter. Buddy had spotted the shiny plane at one time, while the planes were dropping their bombs, but he was too far away to go after him. Also, he, along with Kyle and JR were in a confrontation with some other planes.

By now they had dropped their bombs in Germany, hitting their targets, which was very deep in this country, they flew kind of easy with the bombers on the way back not to use up to much fuel for the return trip and possibly more confrontations which happened on the way back as Kyle, Matt together with Andy following, took down two more German fighters, so it was a very eventful flight.

As they returned to the area where the other planes turned back to refuel we met them again. There were a few more skirmishes, but from here on the bombers were well protected, both here and in Germany. They all headed back to their bases also their debriefing. Buddy was extremely thankful that he hadn't lost anyone also they had their first combat mission under there belts. The next combat mission maybe will not be any easier, but at least they'll know what to expect.

Later after everything settled down Buddy was in the workout room when the other men joined him. He was sure glad to see them working out. It seemed to be that younger men were into working out and building muscles. It was kind of a trend with a new generation. He asked the men how they felt about their first mission each one had a little different perspective. They could tell Tony was more nervous about things then the other guys. He learned never to push too hard. It was always better to let things go their own way. There was no doubt in his mind that these men would go the distance, that's all anyone can ask.

So as the days went by with more missions, everything seemed to fall into a pattern. Of course Buddy almost insisted on his men working out sometimes before they went up. This went on week in week out, as they progressed with the missions. Every once in a while the men would say enough is enough, let's go have some drinks, relax for a while, Buddy and Whip would both laugh.

By now, Buddy realized who was the hunters and hunted it doesn't take long to see how people react in combat, you can sure tell these men had been trained by CT. They went right by the book, which was really good because he knew exactly what they would do. Several times when they came back Tony saw holes in his plane he would turn kind of pale. The other men realized how close they came almost taking it in stride, but then realizing this is war. When they had some down time Buddy would be able to work with them showing them how to evade also use the plane with its speed and being more maneuverable taking advantage of that. There were even times when he would take them up, showing them, how to attack and evade sometimes a little different than what books say. Matt asked him how to do an outside loop, of course, he was told only to do this in extreme measures. Buddy was sure that Matt would probably be the only one of the group that would be able to pull this off. So they covered it as much as they could. It seemed like every time they went up and came back they had more confidence in their flying even Andy became more aggressive, but not like the other three. Sometimes while they were escorting the bombers, Buddy would go off by himself the other four would watch closely, he would act like his plane was not flying very well then, a couple of the enemy planes would come after him, then he would lead them right to the other Mustangs, which in turn would come to annihilate the German planes. This seemed to work good even Tony would get in on some of this. More and more Buddy would go off by himself. Let the four of them wing man each other. One time while they were in Germany He and Wolf met head-on. They both banked around, coming after each other. They got in a tight circle when Buddy's plane started to gain on Wolf, putting a few rounds in his tail Wolf realized this Mustang was faster than his. He quickly broke off, then dove down after the bombers catching one on the way down Buddy was right after him, but had to break off almost crashing into one of the bombers, then lost sight of

Wolf and was engaged by two enemy fighters, one of which managed to get close enough to throw some rounds at him about that time, two other Mustangs came in to help. Buddy did an over the top maneuver and was able to finally take the one FW off his tail. The other two Mustangs must have taken care of the other FW. About that time they all broke off to follow at least 60 bombers after they had dropped their bombs again, hitting their targets. Looking down, he could see the devastation that they had caused to their targets he knew by looking it was mostly industrial areas. He often wondered what kind of materials or what they were working on down there. They sure won't be working on them anymore, thanks to the bombers. They were sure taking their toll on Germany, along with all the other bombers. They were hitting their resources, fuel dumps then hitting Berlin, just about every sector of Germany. Some of the bombers were still getting hit by antiaircraft guns. So part of our duties were to go down to pick them out strafing them as much as we could. Also, any time you saw trains going down the track you went after them. Sometimes you would hit some explosives then almost the whole train would blow up. Mainly we were after the anti-aircraft guns. Sometimes you could only see them when they were going off shooting at our bombers. They would try to hide them in places hard to see. However, we were taking a toll on them also. One day, just coming into German territory where things had been fairly quiet all hell broke loose on one side of Buddy. He knew it was that shiny plane it was coming right in at them, hitting Kyle's plane right beside him. Kyle's plane took a fast nosedive going down in flames. It was Wolf, Buddy lost sight of him because there were several other planes coming in on them at the same time right behind Wolf, so they were all engaged in this skirmish Wolf went on to do his hit and run tactic he liked to do so often, of course, this really got to Buddy feeling responsible, having not protected Kyle, letting the Germans get the jump on him. He went into an extremely personal aggressive state took out two of the remaining planes himself. Then went high to see if he could find Wolf, this was his first loss like this. But then he went back down to protect the bombers also the rest of his crew. He knew he couldn't do anything about it his mission was clear. Get the bombers there so they can do their job. Take care of your personal Vendetta at a later time. After several confrontations that day they made it back to the base, Buddy was really taken back by what happened. Also the other three men were clearly shaken along with him. They all felt like they should've been able to do something to prevent what happened. But there again, it is war. After debriefing Maj. Harrison came to him and said I know what it's like there's nothing anyone can say or do that will help you have to accept this, we are in a real fighting battle out there. There's nothing more dangerous than what we are doing. We all lose men it will tear you apart. Every time you go up, you will try to make decisions that will prevent this, but it is inevitable. Buddy thanked him for what he said of course the wounds were still fresh the memories were still strong. He could only imagine how many men the major had lost. Buddy sat down to write Kyle's family. He felt this was only right that he wrote the letter. He was in charge of this small group. Afterwards, he knew there was nothing he or anyone else could do to help, so the next best thing to do was run, he sure did it seemed like it took the edge off some of the pain but not the memory, as he ran he felt somebody running beside him. He looked over it was Whip the one person that would always be there for him, he always appreciated it. No words were spoken between them they just ran and ran until the sweat was pouring off both of them when they got done Buddy turned to Whip, saying thanks I really needed that Whip replied. I figured you did with that he reached up and tapped on the captain bars saying I'm sure glad I don't have those, along with the responsibility that comes with them. Buddy replied back it is not all what it's cracked up to be as he tapped Whip on the side of his arm a little emotional, saying thanks again. I know I'm repeating myself, so cut me a little slack right now okay. They both got a light smile on their face. Buddy, had a fitful night of sleep off and on he could see the plane in flames beside him that is something you don't get out of your mind very easy. He woke up then setting on the side of his bed with his head in his hands, wondering to himself what went wrong. How did they not pick up on what happened. He knew they were watching intently they always did, then it dawned on him they did not come from up above. They came from down below. We weren't watching for that because they always attacked from up above for the speed to attack, but this time they came from a lower angle and behind us, not seeing them until the last minute, catching us off guard. Wolf knew they were at a disadvantage now with the new planes we had. So they had to attack in a different way just like they did. Buddy was kind of excited about figuring this out because it had been on his mind how they were able to jump them like they did. From now on they would really have to watch what was happening in all directions, high and low. The next day at briefing, he brought this up to everyone plus had it sent out to all divisions. Come to find out this had happened to other groups. From now on, Buddy was biding his time and knew eventually he would have a chance to go after Wolf he stayed tight with the other fighters for now, having lost one man he would pair up with one of the other pilots. It was usually Matt, JR, then Buddy with Andy, that's how it went. Weeks went by, with confrontations both in France and Germany. Every once in a while he would see Wolf with his shiny plane come up, hit and run. That was the way he was going to play it from now on. Sometimes they would send up a whole bunch of fighters from different directions, trying to confuse us but Germany was losing more fighters they were using younger pilots, not as experienced they had used all of their best pilots up by now. We were back to doing a lot of strafing for anti-aircraft guns. But he never lost his cool playing it by the book. There were times when he would let his three men fly together then he would go out to bait a couple younger German pilots bring them in then his men would jump them, this .always seem to work very good. Wolf would always evade any real battles with the P 51's. He realized they were a lot faster and more maneuverable then his FW, so he would just come up, hit and run Wolf would enjoy going at it with other fighters even maybe one of the P 51's. But if two or three Mustangs would come after him, or that Yank he figured he'd be in trouble. So this is the way things went. Buddy would just concentrate on protecting the bombers.

CHAPTER THIRTEEN

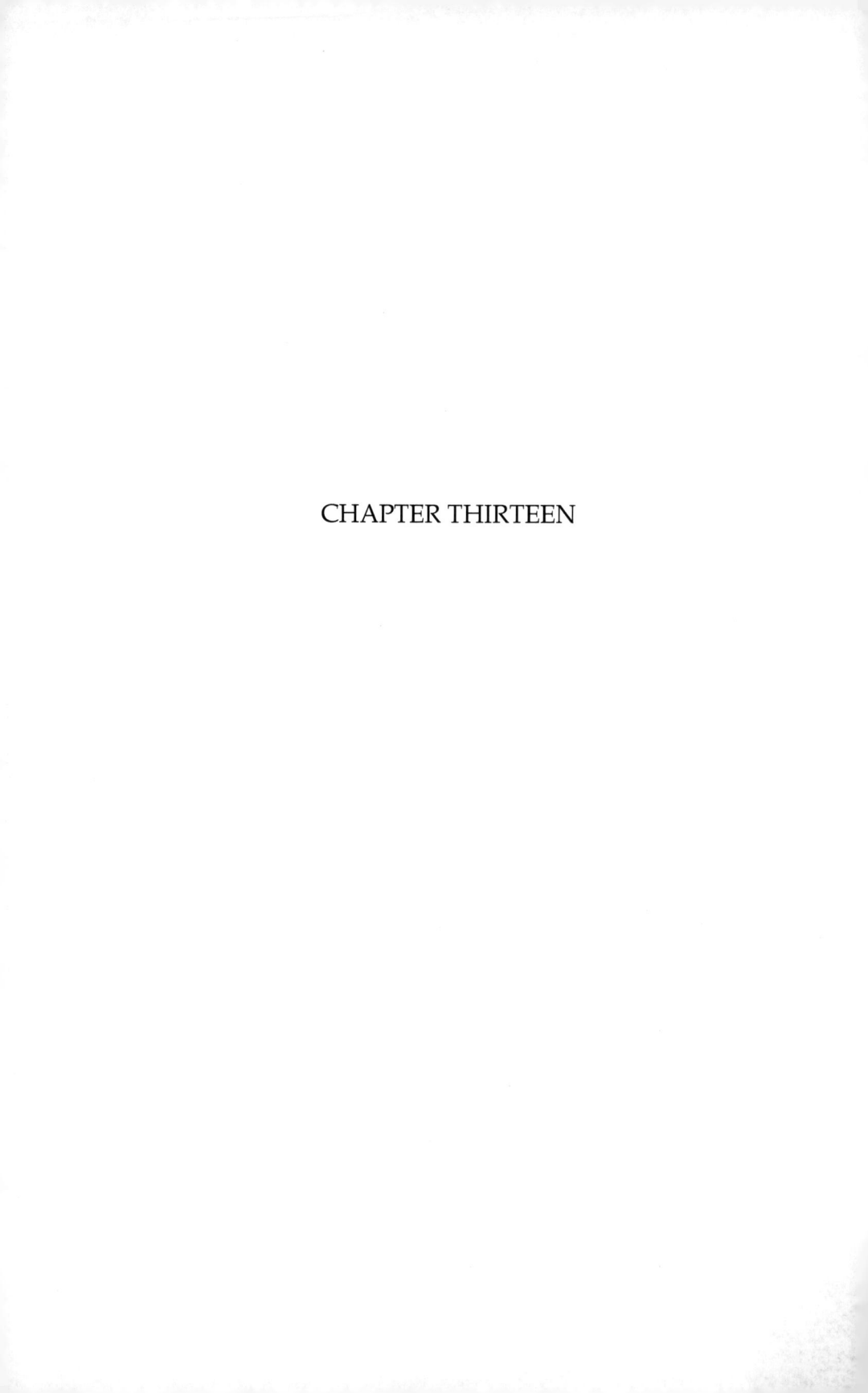

Germany was losing a lot of ground on all sides. The pressure was on from the Russians also the invasion of Normandy. It was basically the beginning of the end. There had also been several attempts on his life to bad they hadn't accomplished this. It would have saved a lot of lives. Hitler was grasping at straws. He was trying everything he could to defend Germany also his occupied territory. They were also running out of fuel and raw materials, so his planes could only stay up for a limited time, also a lot less of them. He did however try to get the Jets up as much as possible, because the bombers were doing such destruction to his country, their main priority was to shoot down as many bombers as they could, but every time they sent one of those jet fighters up, we would concentrate our planes to try to stop them however, as fast as they were It was difficult. They heard that one of our planes had actually followed a jet fighter back to its base, and as it slowed down to land our pilot drilled him right into the ground. Of course, he was in a lot of trouble because of where he was so it was a matter of getting out of their right now. A loud cheer went up when everyone heard that one, then you would hear other cases where our fighters ganged up and were lucky enough to shoot one down, so it was becoming more and more possible to stop them. One day not long after crossing the channel into French territory. Our planes were jumped by some German fighters out of nowhere in the midst of the battle there was a blur across the sky. This kind of shocked everyone realizing that the jet fighter was back in France. So while our planes were fighting off the other planes. The jet would come in to take out as many bombers, as he could. All indications were that Wolf had gained control of the jet fighter again so he was doing his hit-and-run tactics on our bombers however if any of our fighters happened to be near he never hesitated to take them out also Wolf had convinced the upper Nazi echelon to take more fighter planes into France to stop the bombers. the higher echelon had to admit that Wolf was right the first time he did this. It was quite a struggle to get the fuel also the supplies but he managed. The P 51s were taken their toll on the German fighters now that they were able to escort the bombers into Germany and back, put Germany in a very defensive mode. Wolf had ulterior motives to get back into France. He wanted to deal with the farmer and his daughter he was convinced now that the Yank was back, that they had helped him somehow to escape. However, there was no way he could get his jet fighter anywhere near that farm, there was no place to land or take off. So he just had to bide his time to wait for the right situation to arise. He also wanted to get a shot at that Yank, but there was still something bugging him about the whole situation. He wished he could put his finger on, but that would also have to wait. Many times as Buddy flew over France, probably within 100 miles from the farm, his heart would grow warm thinking of Janelle hoping that she and her father were still safe. Many times he'd like to fly down and land just to have a moment with her, to hold her but he didn't dare he could not jeopardize their safety. Now he realized what it meant when guys got letters from home, their girlfriends or wives saying if they could only hold them, even for a short period of time, he sympathized with them Buddy had got a replacement for Kyle. He was sent over from another squadron, his name was Mike he fit in right away with the rest of them also had three kills under his belt. He was on the same level of a fighter pilot like Matt. They were both very aggressive pilots so it was Matt with JR, then Mike and Andy, this left Buddy to pursue what he did best, several times he had got close to the jet fighter, but was unable to actually go at it with him. So the missions continued our bombers were taking their toll, crushing Germany. Allied troops were pushing their way through France also from all the other sides. Tanks and heavy armored divisions were taken Italy also the Russians were moving in from the North.

     This particular morning Buddy's excitement level was higher than normal. He didn't know why, but it was there, Whip even picked up on it, teasing Buddy you look like the

Hawk that's going after the Canary today. Buddy laughed saying it could be the other way around you know. All the pilots, along with the ground crew knew something was coming up. They weren't quite sure what, but the ground crew had been working feverishly to repair all the planes that were grounded, they had been notified to get all available planes ready, so at briefing that morning. It was explained that this mission would be among the largest concentrations of bombers they had assembled for quite some time so they wanted all the available fighters in the air. Also that the Germans were making an all-out effort to stop as many bombers as they could before they even got to Germany so they were figuring somewhere in France there would be quite a skirmish between our fighters and bombers against their fighters also to keep an eye out for the jet fighter. The spitfires and hurricanes were to encompass the bombers, Buddy with his group were to merge with other P 51 fighters from other units, they were to intercept the German fighters before they got to the main group. Not long after they had cleared the channel gaining altitude Buddy was amazed at the bombers Eighth Air Force along with other bombers, the sky was a huge blanket of bombers with other fighters, so everyone got to their places, the P 51s climbing higher gaining altitude, it seem like as far as he could see there were airplanes. It was an amazing sight then Buddy saw some specs in the sky, quickly calling it in someone else also spotted some. There were a lot of bandits up there today just like they said at briefing, it didn't take long before they were all involved in some skirmishes, planes started going down all over the place. Some of the enemy planes had got close to the bombers where the spitfires and hurricanes were fighting with them, Buddy with his group were in a dogfight of their own at this time he decided to get them going in a circle, which was beneficial for the P 51. It could turn sharper also it was faster. There were a lot of bullets flying all over the place, even Buddy felt a few thuds on his fuselage, but so far everything was good. He wasn't losing speed or altitude by tightening the circle he was able to gain on the enemy plane in front of him then taking him down. This also happened in front of him where the other P 51, took down another plane. It was easy to bait the younger inexperienced German pilots into a circle, then once you get them into the circle you could close in on them. The younger German pilots were all too eager to come in behind the P 51. Hoping to knock it down so they could brag about it, but it never seemed to work that way for them. They would inevitably go down in flames. Buddy leveled off, right away he spotted a couple of FWS headed for the bombers, not far from him, so he with two of his group they went in pursuit, soon they started catching up with the enemy planes, then he noticed a small amount of smoke in his cockpit. He motioned for the other two to go after the FWS. He wanted to check out his plane all his instruments read okay, he wasn't losing any power everything seemed to be working fine. He did a few maneuvers to make sure everything responded just right, although he was experiencing more smoke in the cockpit. He knew sooner or later you have to open the canopy in training they had covered this, they made you fly, sometimes with open canopy's to get used to it in case this did happen, the rush of air was very distracting when you first do it specially at the speed you're going at also the altitude, it would help clear the smoke out, then you could close the canopy again he tried this, but again, the inside of canopy started filling up with smoke it was very distracting while he was doing all this he noticed that some of the bombers were exposed because our fighters were in a confrontation with the German planes, then the blur came, not far from were Buddy was, so the bombers got hit, one was able to turn around and head back toward the channel another one went down. Buddy knew he had to get down there to protect those bombers so with his canopy open he came down beside the bombers to protect their flank. Flight commander Harrison was yelling orders for some of our fighters to get down closer to the bombers.

However, a lot of our fighters were in confrontations with the enemy planes. There was a lot of chatter on the radio.
Buddy felt something tugging at his neck. He realized that, the scarf was outside the canopy. He wasn't able to take it off so he loosened it some more. Now the end of the scarf was hanging outside the canopy even more, then, someone yelled out, here comes the jet again from your right side bullets hit the plane in front of him, also one of the bombers, Buddy instantly hit the alcohol injector that he and Axle had installed as his plane leapt forward, Buddy automatically fired in the direction of the jet fighter. It was hard to tell if any of his rounds hit the fighter. This all happened so fast. Within seconds the jet was gone again. Buddy moved his plane forward to be in a better position when Wolf came back. It wasn't long before he came back. Wolf realized that after he had knocked down some of those bombers that this P 51 he was after was the American that he had wanted to kill all this time, he recognized all the swastikas and other images on the side of the Yanks fuselage. He knew that this Yank was not about to run away from him. Wolf was feeling very sure of himself, this time he would have his revenge, but as he shot at the Yank he was surprised at the speed of the P 51. Also, there was something hanging outside the cockpit that grabbed Wolf's attention. It was the scarf. Wolf was kind of confused as to why this scarf was so important to him for several seconds he dwelled on it, but he could not figure it out what did it mean, then it dawned on him that the scarf he saw on the Yank at the prison camp it was the same color scarf he was wearing. It wasn't so much the color, but the way the tassels were made. They were identical to the one he was wearing for an instant Wolf reached down picked up the end of his scarf to check the tassels to Wolf's mind they were identical. This confused Wolf, wondering how could this be, also how did this yank get hold of that scarf, as far as he knew there was only two. The one he was wearing also the one he had lost in Canada. He was sure the girl had taken. By now the Wolf

realized he was running low on fuel, but was not about to give up. He knew he had enough to stay up for a few more passes now more than ever he wanted that Yank, but there was still something nagging him about the scarf. What was so important about it to him then he realized in a split second that, the scarf he had lost had something to do with that girl in Canada he had his way with, she had taken the scarf. He was sure of it, what could this mean, what does this have to do with this pilot could this be her son? He also remembered what he looked like it was almost like looking in a mirror the resemblance was uncanny something started to tug at his mind. Could this have happened could this be his son. Then he realized that this Yank would not hesitate to kill him also he would not hesitate to kill this American, no matter who he was, it was going to be "kill or be killed". There was no other way for these two. Okay, the Wolf said to himself the Yank will die. I will make sure of that. That's where Wolf made his mistake. He hesitated too long at the speed he was going he was coming up on Buddy ready to squeeze the trigger, but it was too late. He overshot the yank by the time he squeezes the trigger the canons went off he was already in front of Buddy's plane, but that was okay. He knew he had enough time to come back around to get him for sure, this time there was no way this P 51, with this Yank could outrun him or even catch him. This revenge would be sweet for what he had done to Wolf's lifetime friend then humiliated him in that prison camp. Wolf only hoped that this yank would have to bailout then the Wolf could toy with him as he parachuted down where he could have his sweet revenge Buddy was waiting for this moment as the jet fighter came in on him. He had maneuvered around, but he was right in the sights of Wolf's guns, but they didn't go off. Buddy didn't wait he already had his finger on the trigger ready for the jet as the plane got near him. He saw the flames coming out of the guns of the jet plane, but they were in front of the P51, Buddy could not understand what had happened, but he didn't hesitate to fire.

Buddy opened up with everything he had, even a few seconds before the jet got in front of his range bullets were already coming out of his guns and the plane was engulfed, smoke started pouring out Wolf's plane. Buddy's heart was racing his adrenaline was running wild. It was hard for him to catch his breath, but he kept right on the trigger. He noticed the jet slightly shutter then slow down. Buddy hit the alcohol button one more time which gave him a burst of speed to come in behind also to the right side of the jet, Buddy kept throwing more rounds at him. Then he let up on the trigger he wasn't sure how much ammo he had left, by now fire was coming out of the jet, as it started to come apart. It was for sure that this jet fighter was on its way to the ground. Then the plane suddenly rolled over upside down, Buddy was following the plane on its way down. He saw the canopy open Buddy fired again to make sure that this plane was going to die. Something came out of the cockpit. It was somebody in a parachute. This was Wolf, his parachute opened he kind of just hung there. Buddy eased the throttle back slowing his plane down. He wanted to make sure this was Wolf, as he came around to the front. He recognized Wolf his whole right side was bloody. It looked like his one arm was just barely hanging there, then he swung the plane around again. He had Wolf in his sights. All he had to do was pull the trigger an Wolf would've disintegrated, but he just could not do that. He knew that a lot of people wouldn't have blamed him for doing it, but he couldn't. Wolf's one arm was raised with a fist he was screaming, probably obscenities Buddy still circling around, did not realize at this time where he was. He was so caught up in the heat of the moment, he was actually circling the farm where he had crashed his plane before there were still sights of a burned-out wreckage, Buddy's heart started racing. If he could just land this plane for a moment and grab Janelle in his arms just to savor the feel of her against him, but of course he couldn't. He still didn't dare to take a chance to expose her or her father, the Germans still occupied this part of the country he could only imagine what the Germans would do to them.

Buddy began to realize what had just happened. Not only this was the end of his archenemy, but one of his missions also to take out the jet fighter that was causing so much damage to the bombers, they had basically eliminated most of the enemy planes in this area. However, he could not celebrate yet the relief feeling had not hit him. Although his excitement level was extremely high he was sure that the life that person laying on the ground now was soon to be over, maybe it had already happened. He knew for sure, this person would never fly again, even if there was such a miracle that he lived through this. As the parachute hit the ground under some trees Buddy could not see in the trees where he was at. Buddy did see some movement though. He could see someone standing there, he made several passes around. He just could not figure out who it was. Then he was able to make out a figure a very large figure there is only one man he knew that large. Buddy got a smile on his face as he flew down dipping his wings several times Then he realized that his plane was still smoking, and decided he better get back up to head to the base before anything else happened. There had been a lot of chatter on the radio there was excitement hoops and hollers everyone was sure that was the end of an evil person. Someone even yelled out, the Hawk took out the Canary, of course Buddy knew who that was, he could hear Whips voice over the rest of them. By now the bombers along with the P 51s had moved on, he was not about to go chasing after them with his plane smoking like it was. Some of the spitfires and hurricanes had turned back for refueling. But some of the guys he was flying with stayed back circling to make sure he was okay. They didn't want anything to happen to the Hawk today, even commander Harrison held back. As they headed back toward the base Buddy's plane sputtered a few times, he wanted more than anything to bring his Mustang back intact and land it. It would be a great symbol of accomplishment to do this. As they crossed the English Channel Buddy's excitement level increased dramatically, something came over him suddenly he couldn't quite figure out what. He knew he was smiling inside and outside there was no doubt in his mind now that Wolf had died. Buddy had some peacefulness about him. He couldn't quite explain it, whatever this was it had to do with when his uncle had told him what had happened to his mother Buddy had made a vow then to get revenge and he did just that. Buddy reached up to touch his scarf only to realize that it was gone he must've lost it in the skirmish. Then he remembered that when he was going down after Wolf's parachute, the scarf was tightening around his neck. He remembered reaching up to loosen the scarf the best he could figure it must have flown out of the cockpit. It did not matter anymore the saga of the Scarlet Scarf was over for him he only hoped this would help his mother in some way. Wolf knew he had made a mistake. Also that he had been hit hard when his plane shuddered as his forward momentum had slowed down then more rounds came through into his cockpit. He felt terrible pain in his right side, his arm along with his shoulder, his fighter got hit again this Yank was really pounding him just exactly what he would've done if the situation was reversed there would've been no mercy. As his mind remembered what he had taught himself earlier in life. Wolf knew it was kill or be killed. However, Wolf knew he wasn't going to die today his plane was in trouble, he would probably bail out, get to the ground then I will get another plane come back up to finish this once and for all. Wolf flipped the plane upside down and pulled the ejection lever and suddenly a rush of cold air hit him as he fell out of the plane in trying to reach with his arm, but it did not seem to work, so he automatically reached over with his left hand finding the cord he pulled it then he felt a very strong jerk as the parachute opened, the pain was increasing on his right side, probably just a piece of shrapnel in his arm. He would have a medic patch him up so he can get back in his other plane he actually smiled to himself thinking this young American pilot probably thinks he's done something to stop me. I will show him I'll torture him more than ever now. Wolf was really excited. He couldn't wait to get to the ground. He was sure his people would be waiting for him. He watched as Buddy's plane came swooping down at him. He just wondered if this American pilot would kill him while he was parachuting down, he probably didn't have the guts to do that. Some of these Americans were like that, they were soft that showed a weakness. As the plane came down very close to him he saw the pilot stick his arm out with his finger and thumb made like a gun shooting at him like he did in the prison this really infuriated Wolf, so he started screaming obscenities to that Yank, by now he was very close to the ground. He was near some trees, when he hit the ground. He was surprised at the pain he wasn't quite ready for that, he actually landed under the trees. He was wondering where his people were they should've already been there waiting for him, suddenly he felt very nauseous also he felt darkness come over him. There must've been clouds in the sky what Wolf didn't understand this was actually death ebbing at him slowly biting, chewing at his body, Wolf caught his breath. He couldn't understand why the pain was so horrific it was just a small wound, he had never experienced this kind of pain in his life he must've landed on something that made him hurt this bad. Then to his surprise as he looked up, the farmer was standing there staring down at him with a big smile on his face. Wolf instantly yelled at the farmer to go get help. The farmer just stood there, resting on a pitchfork smiling down at him. Wolf decided he had enough of this, he reached for his pistol, but nothing happened for some reason his right arm wouldn't work his hand would not grab the gun, he reached again, knowing that he would get a hold of his gun, then he could shoot this farmer right where he stood. Then he would get up, go to the farmhouse have his way with that girl, that dark-haired daughter of this giant man then he would shoot her, or maybe he should torture her first before killing her yes that's what he would do, now all he had to do was get up off this ground. Wolf could taste something in his mouth. He remembered he had this taste before, it was blood. He was wondering where this blood was coming from, then slowly things started getting dark he did not understand what was happening to him. He knew what he had to do, but he could not move his body or even move his arm or his leg, darkness slowly ebbed at him. He convulsed then there was that devastating pain again. Death was slow coming. He felt something piercing his chest, this pain was even worse than the other one also he couldn't catch his breath. His eyes were open gazing into the sky, he saw the farmer standing overtop of him then a Scarlet scarf fell down from between the trees limbs as it draped across his face Wolf thought to himself I have both scarves now, he gasped for air a couple more times, he was choking on his own blood. Then everything went still, darkness overtook him.

    Jacque stood there for a while, waiting, once he reached down to touch the side of Wolf neck, he felt no pulse. He smiled as he turned to walk away. Then he turned back around to spit on the body as he walked away with the pitchfork he knew he would have to clean it off then could not help smiling again. The farmer watched this battle for awhile earlier the plane had crashed into his field, along with many others as he watched Jacque realized the plane that was following the parachute down had an American insignia on it, as he walked toward the barn the plane came back across the sky dipping his wings several times, it suddenly dawned on him, the scarf around Wolf's neck then the other scarf that came out of the sky was like the one that the American had that they had helped. Excitement rose up in him. This could be the explanation for a lot of things, especially when his daughter had asked him about the scarf. He was sure there was a lot more to the story, but some things are better off left alone. One thing he can hope that it was the American that had gotten Wolf. That would have been ironic. They had never heard anything back on what happened to him but they never did hear anything about the ones that they had helped it was just too dangerous. But for his daughters sake he hoped this was what happened. Walking back up to the barn he heard all-too-familiar sounds from a distance, loud booms like thunder he knew the American and British forces were pushing the Germans back, there had been columns of tanks and heavy armament, along with German troops retreating this made his heart feel good. Also he was concerned about his daughter and his future. Fortunately their farm was a few miles off the main road. They were safe for the time being. Buddy landed and taxied over to his parking area. The other four Mustangs were gone, but the spitfires and hurricanes were all landing to be refueled. Buddy was able to stand up. Because his canopy was open, looked around, there was Whip with a big smile on his face, yelling. You deserve a big hug. Buddy yelled back, you better shave first Whip saluted Buddy, he returned the salute. It was a joyful time of course, by now some of the ground crew with Axle was there. Buddy stepped out on the wing. They all yelled and hollered everyone had been listening to the radio they knew what he had done to Wolf. As Buddy jumped down from the plane he nearly collapsed from the stress of the flight, but was able to stand. Axle said, "Does this deserve a handshake" all Buddy did was smile and put his hand out. He could not say anything right now he had to go to debriefing, but it was well known by the look in his eyes that he had done what they had heard over the radio. Even though the guys flying the spitfires and hurricanes had to go back up to meet the bombers on their way back, they still went to debriefing which was fairly short and sweet. Everybody wanted to celebrate but they had to wait because some of them had to go back up to escort the bombers back, however there would be lots of celebration that night, there would be a lot of toasts to the bringing down of the jet fighter, along with the Wolf, if the guys had anything to do about it Buddy would have a few drinks himself, and maybe even get a little drunk. Whip reserved the right to buy the first round of drinks then remembering a talk they had about the scarf, Whip yelled out they better order more beer for tonight.

CHAPTER FOURTEEN

Paula woke from a sound sleep raising straight up in bed, she probably had another bad dream about Buddy, but this was different she felt a warm fuzzy feeling come over her. Her emotions were running wild she had feelings stirring in her she had never had before. She went to the bathroom and washed her face with cold water, thinking maybe this would snap her out of it. She could not remember having a dream about anything. She had some kind of internal excitement, whatever the feeling it was great. Things were still dark outside. She wasn't sure what time it was. She decided to take a hot shower maybe this would calm her down. She knew she had the next two days off work, so there was no reason for her to get up at this time of the morning. The hot shower only intensified her emotions all she could think about was being with Tom. She dressed quickly drove over to Tom's place. Of course she had a key so she let herself in. Tom was still asleep she still could not believe what she was doing so she undressed, then got into bed with him. Tom turned over with a start it was as if he was dreaming. Then he reached over turned the light on, for a minute he knew he was dreaming, because there was Paula in bed with him. They had laid down together several times when he would hold her after she would get bad news about her son, but this was a lot different she was very seductive in her movements she grabbed Tom pressing herself tightly against him. Tom said what's come over you? Paula replied. I don't know, but it's wonderful. It seems like all my inhibitions are gone. Tom's heart was beating fast. He wasn't quite sure what to do next. He knew what he wanted to do. They had come this far before but always stopped. Tom thought real fast, do you really want this, Paula replied yes. Without hesitating or thinking she said yes, yes ,yes, Tom said, then let's go get married. He pushed her away from him, which was really very hard to do right now. If you want this then let's get married, right now Paula said what do you mean right now. Tom said yeah right now we can drive to the state line and get married we can do that today. Paula started crying with joyful tears saying I don't believe this I'm so excited. Tom made a quick phone call to Jim waking him up out of a sound sleep. He and his wife both were a little unnerved by a call this time of the morning, you always assume the worst. When Jim answered the phone realized it was Tom babbling about he and Paula getting married asking them to go with them. It took a few minutes for Jim to clear his head after just waking up, he said let me talk to my sister. Tom put Paula on the phone Jim asked her what's going on sis, I don't know she replied. All I know is I want to marry him right now. We want you two to go also stand up for us. Jim started to laugh saying yes we will go as he hung up the phone. He turned to his wife laughing he told her the news she had a very shocked expression on her face. Jim said this is a revelation of some kind. It's a Paula revelation put it that way, they're going to get married, they want us to go with them. Nonny instantly got excited, her and Paula had talked quite often about personal things, so she quietly went into the spare bedroom to wake Rose her mother, who had been living there, helping the with the children. Before long they were on their way, now daybreak had started by the time they got to the state line the sun was starting to come up, it was going to be a beautiful day. They had no problems finding a chapel. Tom and Paula were married. Paula was so excited she had to hug everybody, even the minister also his wife, Tom was beside himself. He could hardly choke back the emotions. Jim was also, not in disbelief but just in pure wonder. This is the sister that had taking care of him his whole life. He loved his sister he always wanted to have her fulfill her life. It seemed like maybe this was the beginning it was too bad that Buddy couldn't be here to see this. There was a special bond between Buddy and Tom now to see his mother this happy would have been the highlight of his life. The four of them decided to spend the day and the night there. Nonny called home to make sure the children were okay also to inform her mother that they were going to stay the night. Reservations were made at the hotel for the evening. After everyone was settled into their rooms the women went shopping they had left on the spur of the moment, so Paula wanted something very special to wear that night. She could hardly contain herself right now to wait until tonight. She couldn't believe the wild feelings she was having within her body.   Nonny grabbed Paula's hand, saying I've never seen you like this before, Paula replied. I have never felt like this before. I hope this is normal, yes it is Nonny replied. Jim and Tom had time together while the girls went shopping. Jim mentioned I now have a brother-in-law for sure. Tom said that he wasn't sure what happened, but he knew in his heart that this was different. He had many chances to go out with other women, but just being around Paula, she had a quality he had never found in any other woman, now he was sure glad that he had waited. Tom had a very stressful job training these new men, Paula seem to know just exactly what to do, also to be there for him to confide in. Yes she was well worth waiting for. The hotel had a great dining room by the time the girls got back from shopping they were already for dinner with a few drinks. You could feel the warmth between the newlyweds touching hardly letting go of each other long enough to eat. The hotel furnished a small wedding cake for the newlyweds several other couples said their congratulations and shared in the wedding cake. At one point Jim asked Paula to dance, he asked are you sure this is what you wanted? Jim I have never been happier in my life. I know exactly what I'm doing Jim said what happened, she replied, I have no idea. I woke up out of a sound sleep something came over me. Everything has been very good ever since. As Jim and Paula approached the table Paula made an announcement that they were going to leave. They had business to take care of. She grabbed Tom by his hand pulled him out of his chair, Jim and Nonny got up, gave them hugs and handshakes again sending them on their happy way. When they got back to their room Paula said, you have to give me a few minutes as she went to the bathroom. Tom had lit some candles, then turn on some soft music. He wasn't quite sure how this was going to go, but he was sure ready. Paula emerged from the bathroom. Tom lost his breath. She was the most gorgeous woman he had ever seen she walked up to him. He said are you sure you want to do this, she put her fingers on his mouth, saying softly you talk too much replacing her fingers with her lips. The next day, while they were traveling back home with Jim driving, Paula and Tom were in the backseat smiling, holding each other Jim looked in the rearview mirror Paula had a big smile on her face and winked at him. He knew that everything was all right Jim reached over grabbing Nonny's hand squeezing it she squeezed back. Everything was all right. Paula's mind drifted to Buddy naturally, she could not wait to tell him the good news hoping that he was all right. It was hard to celebrate things here while things were so devastating over there, knowing her son was right in the midst of it all, she knew in her heart he wouldn't have it any other way.

All the guys were celebrating Wolf's death. This actually went on for a few days while they had some down time. As they walked out toward the planes Buddy couldn't believe his eyes. Somebody had come up with some polish, now his plane was the shiniest one of them all. There was also a picture along with the other swastikas about Wolf being strangled by the Hawk, the Wolf's tongue was hanging out his eyeballs were crossed with a big red X through it. Buddy said, I wonder whose bright idea this was. Axle said, I am really proud of that one, they both laughed. Escort was becoming routine. However, you never let your guard down, the last real confrontation they had was when Buddy took Wolf out. Also most of the German fighters were eliminated in this area either we destroyed them all, or the remaining few retreated into Germany. Any opposition wasn't encountered until after we left the French territory. Even then the skirmishes were few most of our losses were from antiaircraft guns. Every time we could we would go down strafing to knock them out. Our bombers were having quite a success, knocking out their industry also fuel production and storage areas. Buddy returned to his bunk area one day noticing several letters laying on his bed for some reason the mail had been delayed for some time, one letter was from his uncle for some reason he opened that one first. Always good to hear from him there was also a note from Nonny and the kids. They had to put their scribbles on the letter Buddy would always get a smile on his face laughing to himself almost like he knew what they were trying to say. He remembered when he returned home the day he got his Capt. Bars, the two kids were standing there at attention saluting him Buddy really loved those two. They somehow took the war away for just a few minutes he would only hope and pray that one day he would have children like this. His thoughts drifted to Janelle he remembered telling her about the children, she would point to him and her make her arm like a cradle he knew by that, she wanted children. The other letter was from his mother telling him all, that what was going on back there, how she hoped he was okay then had to give him some bad news, some of the guys that he grew up with had been killed in the war with Japan. The bad part about war was death it had no conscience it didn't mine who it took. He also heard that after the carriers had been able to get planes close enough, we were able to bomb Tokyo. This seemed to turn the tide against Japan. Buddy saw the other envelope that had been laying there. As he looked at it trying to figure it out there was something different. He repeated to himself several times. Mrs. Paula Gray then his heart started to race, he tore the letter open started reading, his mother and Tom had been married, it was hard to believe this. He couldn't ask for better news about that time, his friend Whip came in to see Buddy. They hadn't seen each other in quite a while. Buddy grabbed Whip like they were dancing. Whip said, we have spent a lot of time together, but if we keep going like this we will have some serious questions to answer. They both laughed, the guys from the other end of the barracks, said can we join in the fun. Buddy said yes, let's all celebrate, Buddy had made a special point of asking the maintenance crew to join them also, they didn't have a lot of maintenance to do now days it was a matter keeping them fueled up and ready to go. Buddy had at that time decided to tell his friend a lot of what had happened. Whip had asked him what had happened to the scarf also, what was that all about. Whip himself had lost his whole family when Germany had bombed his hometown, so he and his friend had both been affected by this war hungry group of Nazis. Whip also knew he had a friend in America when this war was over and if he ever wanted to go there he would be welcomed. But there would be a lot of rebuilding to do in his country when this war was over. Even Maj. Harrison and Col. Morrison had joined in the celebration, informing the men that there'd be several downtime days, so they all took advantage of this information, they all toasted more drinks, someone yelled out "those damned Germans can wait another day for another whipping from us". After Wolf went down it was several hours before a German patrol showed up with several big trucks, they headed down to where that jet had crashed to take every piece of that plane with them, the Germans sure didn't want anybody else getting their hands on that. Part of the patrol started looking for Wolf, the pilot. Jacque standing by the barn stepped out pointed toward the trees where Wolf was laying they picked him up putting him on a stretcher then in an ambulance, they headed down the road toward town. They actually ended up taking Wolf to the prison encampment the only doctor available at that time was a Frenchman. He examined the body of course pronouncing him dead. Then the doctor unbuttoned his flight suit, which was soaked with blood. The report stated that this man had died from loss of blood, which was no big surprise however, the doctor upon closer examination found some puncture wounds in his chest. It did not seem normal. They were equally separated puncture wounds it reminded him of the time he examined the body of one of the local farmers that had tragically fell out of the hayloft on to a pitchfork that had punctured him through his chest into his lungs and through his heart. This was very characteristic of the puncture wounds. He was not sure how this could happen so he did not think it was worth mentioning because he probably died from loss of blood. However, there were small drops of blood on the corner of his mouth, indicating puncture wounds to the lungs while still alive. However, the doctor stayed with his original statement, death caused by loss of blood end of story. Jacque walked into the farmhouse proceeding to tell Janelle what had happened, the plane that crashed had been the German pilot that had attacked her and he was dead. He told her of the scarf that was being worn by the German also another scarf that floated down from the sky, where there was an American plane flying over dipping his wings, the scarves were identical, so didn't the American ware the same scarf, the one you asked me about. It took. Janelle a moment to think this over then she said he was here, her father said yes, I think he shot down the German but now he's gone. You said he dipped his wings, he repeated himself. Yes, he dipped his wings several times. No one had ever done that before. She got very excited telling her father that if Buddy ever had a chance he would fly over dipping his wings to let her know it was him also everything was going to be okay. She was so excited she started dancing around the kitchen tears of joy streaming down her cheeks also, she was very glad that the German pilot was dead. She knew in her heart. If he ever had the chance he would come back to finish what he started with her then probably kill both of them without any remorse. Later as the farmer stood looking out over his fields his heart sank. There were large pieces of airplanes, bombers and fighters that had come down some large holes where bombs had been dropped from the planes returning that had been shot up pretty bad they didn't want to land with the bombs inside them. Jacque wondered how he would ever be able to clean up his fields enough to plant crops again. After using his tractor the last time he left it down by the field it had been damaged by falling debris. He was sure it could not be fixed, the future looked very dim. Maybe he could plant a small garden for food for them. He had buried some food under the barn floor, just in case. He told Janelle they had to go to town. They went straight to the store when they got there, Charles the storekeeper was sure glad to see them. He motioned for them to talk, they went to an area in the store where no one could hear them. Charles begins to tell Jacque that one of the underground group had lost his nerve, somehow or was caught, then tortured had given up names of people who would help with the allies, he didn't know how many names had been given so every one had to be very careful. The Nazis had already killed several of the people also that the front lines were getting closer. There was a lot of Germans retreating through here and things were not very safe at all, they had already killed some French people as they were coming through there were loud noises in the distance. Charles told him it's time to go to the tunnel that they had built underground. They would take some supplies with them Jacque mentioned that he had buried some potatoes and carrots he would go back to the farm to get them. The storekeeper said, ok do this as soon as possible then get back here. Janelle will be safe here with my family. We will go down into the tunnel now, so please hurry, that's exactly what they did. This was real hard for the men to be confined to the small area. They could hear loud noises above them. Sometimes the ground would shake all they had was candlelight, along with a couple lanterns to see with. To them it seemed like forever, but actually it was a couple days and nights. Then things got kind of quiet for a while. Once in a while one of them would sneak out to see what was going on but they still weren't quite sure, after things got quiet for quite a long time the two men decided to venture out. They could see armored vehicles and trucks going by, soldiers walking. These were not German soldiers Jacque asked one of the men, saying "no more Germans", and the answer was "no more Germans". He and Charles both got very excited shaking hands with the soldiers who also had smiles on their faces because they knew this was what it was all about. The two men hurried back down into the tunnel and brought everybody out. It was a joyous time for all of them. Jacque was surprised to see his truck, still standing near, undamaged of course it was an old truck. He and Janelle said there goodbyes. After a few minutes of trying, the truck started up. They headed back to the farm, meeting up with a lot of soldiers, both of them were smiling. He saw some French soldiers and talked with them for a while expressing their joy, about getting their country back from the Germans also they had found out that Paris had been liberated "Viva la France" "viva la France" was being said everywhere. Both Janelle and her father were happy. She started reminiscing. Wondering what life held for them, also what the future would bring. Wondering how this all would work. She knew in her heart Buddy would come back for her. But how would she leave her father, especially with the farm the way it was, however she knew somehow this would all work out in time. As they slowly rounded the bend near their farm both of their hearts sank. The house had been blown apart now how were they going to live, but both of them had been through hard times before. They knew right away what they were going to do. Salvage everything they could from the house then move into the barn, their old stove that they used before had been stored there. The farmer had used it periodically there was a grain room in there big enough to make a place to sleep they had dragged the beds down from the house. They used a couple of tubs for washing and cleaning. She had a way of making things work sometimes he would be down in spirits. She would realize this and had a way of bringing him back up. She was like her mother that way no matter what happened she was always ready to make things better Buddy's group had been flying escort, but when they were not doing that they did a lot of ground support this took him in a different direction for about a month he was not able to get back by the farm, although they knew by reports that this area was where our troops were moving through swiftly. He also knew the French, British and American soldiers had occupied that territory now just possibly if he got back near there he might even be able to land safely. About a week later his wishes come true as he flew over toward that area His heart started racing would he be able to see her and hold her in his arms shake her father's hand. He was almost afraid, then, as he flew over the farm. His heart sank. He couldn't believe what he saw, the farmhouse had been blown apart his mind was running wild he flew over several times dipping his wings. Hoping it would bring somebody out. Certainly as low as he was flying someone would certainly come out to see, no one did so he landed the plane on a small part of the ground that they were using this field to transport men in and out of this area. He knew the prison camp where he had been held wasn't too far away He was sure they had got all the prisoners out by now. After jumping down off the plane Buddy ran up to the farmhouse then into the barn, only to discover no one was there. He saw that they had made some kind of a living area in the barn that meant they were Ok then. But where were they now, many questions. He knew that they had gone to town at times mostly her father, but he would not know who to talk to in town also he was sure no one would talk to him about it. He had no other choice but to leave. After landing back at his base, he reported in which there wasn't much to report. He went to see the Maj. asking him if there was anything he could do to help him find out what had happened to them. The Major did not know firsthand what had happened. He knew that those particular people had helped a lot of crews, and pilots so they had been taken to a place here in England. There was conflicting reports coming in of their whereabouts, but he would do whatever he could to find out. Buddy thanked him. The next few weeks were more or less, routine. but lord help any of the German fighters that might show up on the horizon anywhere. Buddy's revenge was very swift, with no mercy. Then he found out that this outfit was being split up the Hurricanes and Spitfires were being transferred to France, where they could escort further into Germany. Buddy's outfit would be reassigned to the Eighth Air Force. It was going to be quite an emotional time they had all become friends with these men, as they said there goodbyes everyone vowed to keep in touch with each other. Whip, told Buddy I don't know how you'll survive without me looking after you. Yeah Buddy said, who is going to run with me when I need to blow off steam also be there for me when I need somebody to talk to, they both laughed, but deep inside their emotional ties ran very deep. Axle, along with his men were packing up their tools to take with them Axle turned to Buddy saying well sir it's been a pleasure keeping your plane flying, lately you've been pushing it a little more then before, yeah Buddy said, I guess I have been in a few jams lately I'm glad you with your men were able to keep me up there while I was blowing off some steam. I sure needed that. Axle I want to keep in touch with you. My uncle really likes your work, every modification that they suggested with your help it made a difference. I am sure when this is over there'll be room for someone like you with your talents at the plant. In fact, my uncle guaranteed you a job there. Axle got very quiet for a minute after this war is over. I don't have much to look forward to my family has all been exterminated by those Nazi bastards. I'll keep doing my best to keep these planes flying an bring this to an end, but I will take you up on your offer, you and I have learned a lot together, I appreciate all you have done. I know you put your life in my hands many times we made sure we did the best we could with what we had we kept them flying didn't we. Buddy handed him a box in a paper bag Axle opened the bag, there was a whole box of cigars, that should keep you busy for a while, that's from all of us back in the states a little thanks. Axle got a big smile on his face. What do you mean a little, that's a lot of thanks Instead of saluting they shook hands. As Buddy turned to head to his plane where the other men were waiting he saw the Col. and the Maj. approaching they proceeded to tell Buddy that most of the French underground that we were able to get out of France were brought here to England, we're not sure where they are. Intelligence is pretty tightlipped about that you can understand why, but they are well guarded as soon as we find out anything different we will let you know, Buddy proceeded to tell both of them what his plans were, that was to get Janelle and her father to the states he wanted to marry Janelle here, Col. Morrison said that if and when this happens he would do everything in his power to expedite the paperwork. Buddy said thank you for everything. With that they joined the other pilots, saying their goodbyes. Both the Maj. And the Col. expressed their gratitude for their support and a job well done. They all snapped to attention then saluted. The 5 P51 Mustangs took off from this field for the last time. They flew for about 100 miles to their new destination, attached to the Eighth Air Force. It took several days for Buddy to get settled in along with the other four pilots. He was getting accustomed to the base. They were doing escorts from the base also settled into a good routine. Buddy was able to have someone transport all the workout equipment to this base where there was a building provided for them for all their equipment, the fighters were separated from the bombers. They even had their own runway. He saw an area that was black top, it wasn't being used much anymore this would be a perfect place to jog, quite a few men were taking advantage of that area. Buddy had been jogging for a few days when he noticed an area off to one side. That seemed to be more heavily guarded than the rest of the base. It caught his interest, so he jogged over to the fence. He was instantly confronted by armed soldiers. As he looked through the fence he could see they were civilians, he recognized one of the men inside the encampment he caught his breath. He did not know too many men that were as big as that person. Buddy was escorted to the entrance where he was thoroughly questioned upon producing his ID the Capt. in charge of security made a few phone calls to verify who he was. The Capt. stood up, reached out to shake Buddy's hand saying, so you are the Hawk that got the Canary, the Capt. smiled, Buddy acknowledged with a smile and handshake. The Capt. said, you must understand the security here. We take no chances with anyone so what is your reason for being here. Buddy explained the situation realized that this Capt. was part of intelligence and could be trusted. The Capt. listened intently, then saying, you still have to fill out some forms. Buddy replied. I'll do whatever it takes. While he was filling out the forms the phone rang again. After listening, on the phone for a few minutes, the Capt. said yes Sir, as he hung up. He turned to Buddy with a smile saying that came from very high up vouching for you. So without hesitation, the Capt. escorted him into the compound and said you're on your own, as Buddy came around the end of one building. He saw Janelle with her father. She turned with a look of disbelief on her face. Within a second, she flew to him. They were in each other's arms. There were tears of joy, her father came up to them putting his arms around both of them. After what seemed like an eternity they were able to tell each other stories on how they came to be there, back in the office where the Capt. was waiting for them, there were more forms to fill out the hardest thing was for them to separate again for a short period of time every minute Buddy wasn't flying he was with them. Buddy explained to them what he had done about buying a farm not far from the base. It had all the necessary farm equipment all it needed was somebody to use it. When Jacque heard that news he knew his prayers had been answered. One thing about it crops didn't care what language you spoke. Buddy and Janelle were married in a small chapel on the base. This would also help expedite the paperwork. Buddy wanted to make sure that if anything did happen to him by being married she was entitled to all the benefits also would be well taken care of. Buddy's dream had come true. It wasn't very long until Janelle and her father were on their way to a new life. Buddy knew that when he got back to the states that there would be a large double wedding.

Tom had some exciting news of course he had access to information which was a lot faster than the mail which he was sure that Buddy would write to tell everyone. Paula was overjoyed to hear the news she kind of knew that this might happen, so she had started taking a class in French. She couldn't wait to put her arms around both of them when they arrived and welcome them to their new home.

Made in the USA
Columbia, SC
28 January 2023